CALLUM
AND THE
OTHER

Alan McClure

Beaten Track
www.beatentrackpublishing.com

Callum and The Other

First published 2022 by Beaten Track Publishing
Copyright © 2022 Alan McClure

Paperback ISBN: 978 1 78645 530 7
eBook ISBN: 978 1 78645 531 4

Cover design by Debbie McGowan

Beaten Track Publishing,
Burscough, Lancashire.
www.beatentrackpublishing.com

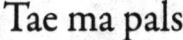

Tae ma pals

Contents

CALLUM
AND THE
OTHER

Bus

H ERE'S A SCENE, look: fourteen-year-old Callum Maxwell, back of the school bus, head rocking in time as it bumps down the long road back to Skerrils. It's a glowering day outside, low clouds covering the Mountain, and Callum feels as dreich and waesome as the rolling boggy land they're traversing.

Four rows in front of him, his old pal Steven is standing nonchalantly in the aisle and talking too loud to a group of lassies, no doubt bragging about football or shinty or swimming or something. The girls are rolling their eyes but they're still listening, laughing when they're supposed to, and though Callum is trying to zone it all out he can't help but envy Steven's easy confidence.

The bus is a shoogly, rattly old rustbucket so he can't make out the patter, can't pick up any tips: not that he really wants to. In the last year or so, Steven has decided that the lassies of Skerrils are the prize in some kind of game, and the chat he has with them is just one of the moves. He goes at this with the same determination that used to see him building boats to sail to MacArthur's Island, but this new obsession is nowhere near as much fun to join in with. Callum, glaikit wee laddie that he is, still sees girls as actual people and has the silly notion that a conversation should be *about* something. Frustratingly, most of the girls seem to prefer Steven's approach, and they've little time for the daydreamy wee bletherskite at the back of the bus.

Not for the first time today, or indeed this journey, Callum really misses Vicky. A scholarship to a music school hundreds of miles up north has robbed him of his best friend, and while he's glad for her and knows she deserves it, he could do with her telling him not to be daft as he worries about the way things have changed.

He peers out the window. The bus is passing a couple of BT vans parked in a layby, the workers standing in their hi-vis jackets, looking glum. Callum raises a hand to them but they just stare blankly back, and then they're gone, disappeared in the mist. *No very friendly,* thinks Callum, then gives a shudder. The damp and dingy distance is seeping into his bones and he wishes the bus would hurry up. The driver, Eric, never seems to take the thing out of third gear, responding to the regular shouts of teenage frustration with a good humoured, "If ye want tae gang faster, get yer ain bus!" So Callum knows there's nothing for it but to be patient.

Truth be told, he misses Steven too. When it's just the pair of them together, things are still grand. They have a laugh, watch a bit of telly, complain about Mr. Blackwell the history teacher, make daft plans that they'll never execute. But when there's other folk around, Steven's a different person. He even puts on a different voice, louder, deeper (though still not very deep; he is only fourteen, after all), and he gets all cool and aloof with Callum.

At first this made Callum want to chin him, but as time's gone on it just makes him feel discouraged and abandoned. He fantasises about the bus rolling over, a dreadful accident, crawling from the wreckage. He realises there are people trapped in there, and throwing caution to the wind he climbs back in, flames licking round him, dragging them all to safety. Last of all, an unconscious Steven, who only comes to when he's safely laid out on the grassy verge, Callum tending him stoically. Bruised and charred, Steven finally remembers who his real friends are and he apologises tearfully for his foolishness, suggests a camping trip on MacArthur's Island, and, and...

And Callum scolds himself for this nonsense. It's exactly this sort of silly make-believe that makes him an embarrassment to Steven, no doubt. Everyone else left these sorts of games behind when they went up to the Academy, but for some reason, Callum can't seem to. He's stuck between two worlds. There was one in which he was special, had achieved something amazing (though no-one can remember exactly what that was) and there's one where he's just another daft wee laddie from the sticks, jostling down crowded corridors in a giant school an hour away from home. Is it any wonder he's in no hurry to make the transition?

The bus rattles over the final cattle grid. Callum should be happy, should be filled to the brim with plans and schemes, two weeks of October holiday and the whole of Skerrils at his disposal. The sea, still just about swimmable on a clear day, the Old Wood, the Holy Cairn, the monument, the Mountain...

But even Skerrils isn't what it was. On the surface, nothing's changed. Heck, nothing ever changes. But only on the surface. For Callum at least, Skerrils lost its beating heart on the sweet spring night when Papa passed away, seated in a garden chair, an unlit pipe in his hand and cherry blossoms drifting and twirling to the ground around him. Callum's mum had been by his side. She said later that his eyes just closed, he smiled, and sighed, and left the world behind. Everyone agreed it was as good a passing as a man could wish for. But it was still a passing.

It had not been unexpected. The old man had never quite regained his strength after the heart attack, and for his last couple of months he'd hardly had the energy to keep up a conversation. Even that hadn't mattered too much to Callum; there was so much between them that didn't need said that it had still been wonderful just to sit in his company, have questions answered with a low chuckle, to look into those old, smiling eyes and know how close they would always be. And then, too soon, he was gone.

Suddenly, Eric the driver slams on the brakes and Callum is pitched forward, his nose making sharp contact with the seat in front.

"*Ow*, ya wee..." He manages to stifle a rude word, partly due to good manners and partly because he's secretly delighted to notice that Steven has been knocked clear off his feet and is now sprawling in a clumsy sweary heap at the lassies' feet. Better still, the girls are finding this at least as funny as Callum is, one or two even filming the spectacle on their phones.

Callum jumps to his feet, feeling a bit guilty for laughing, and goes to give Steven a hand. As he heads down the aisle, he peers through the windscreen to see why they've stopped and is instantly arrested by a troubling sight. Standing in the middle of the road, oblivious to the bus despite Eric's musical and insistent use of the horn, is the strange old man who has been hanging around the village since the late summer. Though small and frail, the man always seems to occupy a space much bigger than himself, like a bare, wintry tree surrounded by the ghost of summer leaves.

He has been the oddest presence in Skerrils because no-one has any explanation of who he is or how he came to be amongst them, and the time is now long past when it might be polite to find out. Adults cross the road to avoid him, shushing the questions of their curious children and pretending nothing is amiss. Stories have started to pile around the old man's bent shoulders like snowdrifts around a dyke, but really, no-one is any the wiser. He makes his painful way around the town uninterrupted, tap-tap-tapping with his gnarly old cane and gazing at some distant horizon invisible to anyone but himself. Callum has long decided that he's going to get to the bottom of this, but the opportunity has never arisen: he's only ever seen the man in the distance, or through the car window as the family drives off somewhere. Maybe the holidays will offer a chance.

"'Sake..." splutters Steven from the floor, grudgingly grabbing Callum's offered hand and struggling to his feet. "Ye trying to kill us or what, Eric? Thanks," he adds to Callum with a quick grin, and for a second, he's the old Steven, gallus, garrulous and un-knock-downable.

"Look," says Callum, pointing at the road ahead. The ancient figure has slowly turned and is facing them, but even now, it's hard to tell if he knows they're there.

"Whoa," says Steven. "Him!"

"Yep," says Callum. "It's lucky Eric drives at fifteen miles an hour, or he could have been killed!"

Steven laughs, but nervously. "Aye, well," he says, "maybe not. You cannae kill a ghost, you know."

At this point, Eric, with a crunch of gears and a muttered curse, throws the bus into reverse and heads noisily back up the street.

"Sorry, kids," he calls over his shoulder. "Looks like we're taking a detour!"

And with that, they turn off down Gilmartin Street through the cold, damp evening, the atmosphere even chillier in the dark light of the old man's distant gaze.

Jenny

As the bus edges past a group of phone engineers, Callum hears more angry honking from behind and peers back to see a car, engine revving aggressively, mount the pavement and roar past the irksome figure in the middle of the road. Clearly someone far too important to consider a detour for the sake of some old man. He and Steven look at each other.

"Craig," they say in unison.

Craig, their old friend and companion, is basically a stranger to them now. His dad drives him to and from the school so he needn't endure the indignities of Eric's bus, and when they're at the Academy he's usually surrounded by a new group of friends. Well, 'friends' is maybe too strong a word; Callum's certainly never sensed any friendliness from them, anyway. They're usually to be found behind the technical department in a cloud of sickly smelling vape fumes, spitting through their teeth and passing loud and harsh judgement on anyone who strays into their line of sight. To be fair, Craig himself isn't the one doing the shouting, at least, not at Callum, but he's still there amongst them, swelling their ranks.

Callum's never been quite clear as to why this shower has adopted his old pal, but he's narrowed it down to one of two possibilities: they've either a) been dazzled by his glittering personality, or b) been dazzled by his brand-new iPhone and the fact that he gets dropped off every morning in a shiny BMW with customised licence plate. Either way, having some kind of a crew is probably better than being lonely, but only just.

The streetlights they're passing are flickering on now, each illuminating a halo of mist as the night weighs heavier on the town's tired shoulders. Steven has dusted himself off and is back at the patter, making mock threats to anyone who'd dare post footage of his recent roll in the glaur. Callum's about to return to his seat when he sees something in the gloom outside. The bus has paused to drop someone off and he can see down the narrow alley where Papa used to live.

He hasn't come down here for weeks. He takes different routes through town to avoid it, though he's not entirely sure why. Now, he can't help but look, and to his mingled shock and surprise he sees a muckle great removal van parked outside. Men in overalls are carrying boxes in through Papa's front door, directed by a small, round woman with dark, curly hair.

Before he even knows what he's doing, Callum has yelled at Eric not to pull away, has swiped his schoolbag off the back seat and is leaping off the bus. Trying not to look too frantic, he strides down the alley, turning the collar of his blazer up against the clinging haar, jog-walking to the spot and arriving flustered and breathless.

"Excuse me," he gasps as he arrives at the woman's side. "What's going on?"

He's interrupted her in mid-flow as she explains to one of the men where she wants him to put a hideous lampshade, a thing that looks like a disco ball that's lost a fight with an octopus. The woman turns to face him. Her cheeks are flushed, and she looks a bit harassed, but there's kindness in her eyes as she looks Callum up and down.

"You what, darling?" she says. She has a strong accent, from somewhere down south, Callum guesses. The removal man behind her looks at his watch, and Callum suddenly realises he doesn't really have a plan here.

"Um," he starts cleverly, "sorry, it's just that this is my...I mean, this house is, well, *was*..."

The woman puts a hand on his shoulder and smiles. "Hang on a mo, love," she says. She turns to the removal man and tells him just to stick the lampshade anywhere, then looks back at Callum. "Now then, young man. Would you be Callum, by any chance?"

He nods, dumbly. "And this was your granddad's house, wasn't it?"

"How did you...?"

She holds a finger up to quiet him, then shouts into the house. "Jenny? Jenny, come down here a minute, love!" She gives Callum's shoulder a squeeze. "My daughter," she explains. "We asked if any kids lived here before we bought the place, and the estate agent told us the last owner had a grandson. Jenny was worried the whole village was like a retirement home! Hard enough leaving all your mates without worrying you're gonna be the only kid in the village, know what I mean?"

Well, Callum doesn't really know what she means, but she seems nice, so his initial outrage at anyone trespassing on this sacred ground is diminishing. The woman carries on chatting away, not, apparently, bothered by his lack of response, and he sneaks a glance through the front door. Piles of boxes line the hall, and he can see unfaded rectangles in the wallpaper where Papa's few pictures had hung. He's starting to form a thought about this when a girl of about his own age comes thundering down the stairs and neatly slaloms the cardboard assault course to make her way out onto the street.

"Yeah?" she says to her mum. She is a vision of black and purple, from her tightly laced Doc Martens to her

13

baggy striped jumper. "Oh, hello," she says, noticing Callum.

Suddenly abashed, and inwardly birling at the thought that he should feel so uncomfortable *here*, of all places, Callum holds out a ridiculously formal hand and says, "G...good evening!"

The girl gives a sharp cackle of delight, looks at her mum in disbelief. "Good *evening*? Well, yeah, sure. Good evening!" She gives his hand a friendly slap.

"This is Callum, Jenny," says the woman. "You know, the one Mr. Barnes told us about?"

"Oh, yeah, 'course," says Jenny. "You coming in, Callum?" Without waiting for an answer she turns and heads back in, taking the stairs three at a time and disappearing from view.

Callum, hand still outstretched and mouth open, is shoogled out of his dwam by the reappearance of the removal man. Jenny's mum, who seems to have forgotten about him already, is issuing instructions about a large box labelled CDs/PHOTOS/ COOKING/HATS etc.

Well, why not? he thinks, and heads inside.

Jenny's room used to be what Papa called the boxroom, a sparse, square space with a small, high window. She's already got a bed and a desk set up, and the room is lit by a dozen candles in different-coloured jars. Other than that, it could still be a boxroom; every inch of floor space is taken up with bags and boxes, crates and containers. When Callum comes in, Jenny has returned to sorting through all this junk, and she has her back to him.

"Have a seat," she says without looking round. "Sorry 'bout the mess. We only just got here today!"

"Nae bother," says Callum, sitting on the desk.

Jenny turns to face him. "'Nae bother!'" She laughs. "I love it! *'Ock aye, nae bother, Jimmy!'*"

Callum is banjaxed. "Who's Jimmy?" Then, realising she was making fun of his accent, he protests, "Here, hang on a wee..."

She looks at him expectantly, eyes twinkling mischievously in the candlelight.

"A wee?" she prompts. "A wee, tiny wee sleekit minute, jings aye?" She gives a hoot of such unabashed laughter that Callum can't help joining in, slightly hurt though he is.

"Jeezo," he says. "You're no shy, are you?"

"Oh, sorry," she says. "I'm not taking the mick, honest. My granny was Scottish. I love it, really. But it might take a while to learn how to speak Scottish proper!"

Callum's about to advise her not to bother trying when she changes the subject.

"Sorry about your granddad, by the way." She hops onto the bed and crosses her legs. "Really sorry. That's harsh, losing someone you're that close to."

15

And Callum is filled with the tooth-grindingly embarrassing certainty that he's about to cry, in front of this complete stranger. He can't think why. Perhaps it's being here, in the house, or perhaps it's because the simple tragedy of it hasn't been so clearly summed up by any of his actual friends since it happened. 'Harsh' is exactly what it is. He sniffs and angrily wipes his eyes.

"Yeah. Sorry." His voice is choked. He's angry at himself, angry at this cocky lassie in her candlelit room, just angry at everything.

Jenny fills the gap in the conversation by getting back to her boxes, changing the subject again, blethering about her hometown, her parents' divorce, her plans for the décor. After a while, Callum has forgotten what he was upset about and is able to join in, and before he knows it, half an hour has passed.

"Oh, hell!" he yelps, leaping off the desk. "I was meant to be home ages ago! Sorry, I have to go!"

He swings his bag over his shoulder and heads downstairs, hearing Jenny shouting, "Off you pop, then!" behind him.

As he jogs through the mist for home, he is assailed by two thoughts: firstly, how annoying this new girl in town is; and secondly, how early would be too early to call in for her in the morning?

Mist

THIS MIST, NOW. Can you see there's something strange about it? It swirls and eddies around Callum's shoulders, follows in his wake, clings lovingly to his hair and clothes, forming silver drops of dew that render him luminous in the lamplight. To Callum, right now, it is just an irritation, but to the mist, if you look closely enough, Callum is the most exciting thing to have happened in eons. He's sparked it to life, changed it from a shapeless grey mass to a spinning, skinkling galaxy of dancers, each tiny particle drawn to him like pilgrims to a shrine. To them he is colossal, surging through them like a tanker through the waves, though together they are a swallowing cloud in which he all but disappears. They love him, court him, but he remains oblivious, intent on getting home.

Now you may think this is just how mist behaves, and perhaps you'll see it yourself the next time you sally forth on a foggy day. And certainly, it parts and swirls as gleefully around the passing cars, the huddled jackdaws on their chimney pots, the boats in the harbour that tip and turn on the swell of the rising tide. But the way it follows Callum, it's like it's wanting to be seen, like it's trying to catch a friend's attention.

For now, though, Callum is as blind to past friendships as Steven or Craig have ever been, and the message is carried sadly on the currents of air as he makes his way through the town.

Faster than texting, faster than thought, the word goes out. *He is still lost to us.* It rides the waves of the atmosphere and adds a chill to the cold, damp night, a half-felt fear that has the good folks of Skerrils pulling their curtains shut, stoking their stoves, turning up the volume on the early evening telly. *What a night,* they think, not knowing why. *Wouldn't want to be out there on a night like this!*

But one person *is* out there.

Even as Callum finally makes it home, bursts through the front door, yells, "I'm ho-ome! Sorry I'm late!" to his folks and dumps his damp blazer on the floor, there is still one lonely figure in the streets of Skerrils.

The old man is still standing in the middle of the road, stick in hand, back bent. His cloudy eyes have been scanning the distance since before Eric's bus had to brake to avoid blootering him, and they're scanning still. He turns and wavers like a rusty weathervane on a church steeple, waiting, turning, sniffing the air.

He is an arresting sight, this old man. Gnarly as a tree root, twisted and bent, in worn old clothes of hodden grey. There's something faintly military about his long coat, but if it is a uniform, it's a uniform of a long-distant time. He has silver hair under his bunnet and a neat, white, pointed beard. At first glance you'd think him a wise old soul, a man who's weathered many storms and has many tales to tell, but he carries this strange, cold aura around him which has driven everyone away.

As a general rule, the people of Skerrils are not the sorts to leave you to your own devices. Whether out of kindness, nosiness or belligerence, a stranger is a person to be met, conversed with, shown the ropes. Tourists come back year after year because it is a friendly town, a place where people wave to one another as their cars pass in the road, who stand and blether on street corners in the cool, salty breeze. And yet this old man has been avoided, filtered out, ignored. He's spoken *about*, not spoken to, a kind of unchancy thought at the back of the mind that you don't want to take out and air.

And can you see him, now, there in the street? Even the mist avoids him. There is clear, cold air around him as the silvery molecules nudge and jostle to avoid his touch. Those that stray too close are instantly frozen, trapped in hoarfrost to drift, shackled, to the ground. Where they were eager for Callum's attention they seem terrified by this man's cold eyes, his tilting, swivelling stare. Their mournful song at the loss of Callum, their long lament, half-guessed by the town but drowned and blinded by flickering screens, reaches this man's ears as clearly as a foghorn.

Callum is lost, Callum is lost. It chimes and reverberates through the night, a tolling bell, a cry for help, but the only ears that hear it belong to one who will offer no help. Head cocked now for the clearest signal, the old face creases in a cold, cruel smile, the back straightens, the eyes grow dark. And now it is as plain as day that there is nothing kindly, nothing faded, nothing deserving of sympathy or care in this bleak, dark figure.

"So," he says, in a voice like a winter's night, "Maxwell is lost. Then the time is almost upon us." And with that, he turns and strides off, all indecision and frailty gone. He marches off up the high road beyond the reach of Skerrils' dim lamplight and into the swallowing night, while in the town below him our hero joins his parents at the dinner table, scoffs mince and tatties and wonders what the weeks ahead will hold.

Blattering

SATURDAY MORNING, AND Callum wakes from dreams of helicopters to find it's the thundering rain on his skylight he's been hearing. It's still pitch-black outside but his digital clock says half past nine. A Skerrils October in all its glory. Not a thing to make you leap from your scratcher in boundless enthusiasm, but Callum's not one to lie in, so he tumbles, yawning, out of bed. He gets dressed and makes his way downstairs where he finds breakfast laid out and a note from his mum saying they're off out to the garden centre and could he wash up when he's finished.

Digital clocks and handwritten notes—why doesn't he just use his phone like a normal person, you may be wondering? Well, if you'd asked that a few years ago, the answer would be simple: there was no reception anywhere in Skerrils, so owning a phone was largely pointless. It's a different story these days, though. The village has been dragged, kicking and screaming, into the twenty-first century, and thanks to the wonders of fibre-optic cables, nearly everyone can enjoy the delights of the internet on handy, pocket-sized devices.

In fact, believe it or not, Skerrils is at the heart of the digital revolution because Craig's dad was one of the designers of PingMe, the hottest new social media app since the last one. Like all new social media apps, it does exactly what all the other ones do and is chiefly an opportunity to add all the same people to a slightly different platform. The one innovation for which Craig's dad takes credit is that as well as having a profile picture you can also have a profile sound, about three seconds long, and this sound plays every time you post anything. This is exactly as annoying as you'd think, but the novelty hasn't quite worn off yet and uptake around the globe has been huge.

You can record your own sound or buy them from online stores, so a stint on PingMe offers up such treats as three-second snatches of thundering drum and bass followed by classic rock riffs followed by someone farting into a microphone. You can open a private channel with a few friends and, by posting in rhythm, use your sounds to make weird audio collages that no-one in their right mind would ever want to listen to but which most of Callum's acquaintances are inexplicably delighted by.

And yet, for some reason, Callum has yet to climb aboard this bandwagon. In fact—you may need to brace yourselves for this—Callum doesn't actually have a phone. It's not even as if he's not allowed one;

his mum has offered to buy him one so she can check up on him at school. The very idea of this strikes Callum as ridiculous, though. He's survived fourteen years without having to check in with home, and he can see no earthly reason why he'd want to start now.

To be fair, the only person he'd want to keep in touch with is Vicky, and rumour has it that she uses her phone to wedge the window open in her dormitory up north. It was a nice phone, too. Her mum had given it to her as a reward for getting into the music school. Sadly, where Vicky's concerned, if you can't play a tune on it, it might as well not exist. She'd have been happier with two tin cans and a length of string because she could have clattered the cans together and twanged the string.

Anyway, Callum is a phone-free zone, so if he wants to contact people, he has to do it face-to-face. Today, he wants to see Jenny again and find out more about her, so he's going to have to head out through the blattering rain. It's going to be hard to pretend he just happened to be passing, but he supposes he'll have time to think of a reason on the way. He tidies up, grabs his jacket and pushes out the front door. Instantly, he's whammled by the wind, and the rain takes precisely three seconds to work its way through his supposedly waterproof jacket.

This is not the invigorating, life-bringing rain of spring. This feels like someone is trying to power-wash the last trace of summer colours out of the landscape, strip the town back to bare plaster and every living thing down to bone and branch. The sun has just about struggled over the horizon, but it might as well not have bothered. It's practically dark, and there's nothing much worth seeing anyway. Callum doesn't mind getting wet, but it is also bitterly cold, so he hurries through the flowing streets to Papa's—sorry, *Jenny's*—house, trying to get his story straight all the way.

I'll say I'm looking for my dog, he thinks, before realising that it won't take a great deal of investigation for Jenny to discover he hasn't got a dog. *I'll say I think I left my schoolbag there yesterday. No, I'll say I thought she'd want to know where the library is. No, no, that's ridiculous. I'll say it sounded like she was coming down with a cold yesterday, and she should try hot honey and lemon like Mum makes.*

The only upside to all this nonsense is that it's distracting Callum from the fact that he is utterly drookit and completely frozen, wandering half-blind through the streets with the icy rain in his eyes.

I'll say I never caught her mum's name and I was worried about being rude. I'll say I'm looking for my dog. No, I've already tried that one.

Before he knows it, Callum is at the door, so strange and so familiar at the same time. He chaps it three times and waits, still muttering glaikit excuses under his breath. He can hear footsteps bounding downstairs from inside, and for a panicked moment he considers turning to flee in the most pointless game of chickenelly ever played. He's too cold and wet to do anything so swiftly, though, so he's still there when the door swings open to reveal Jenny in panda pyjamas and a striped goony. She looks at him enquiringly.

"Ehm... Morning," he stutters. "I was looking for my—"

"In you come," interrupts Jenny, turning and heading back upstairs and shouting, "Mu-um, Callum's here!"

"Hello, love!" comes echoing from the kitchen, just about audible over the merry rhythm of Radio 6 Music. Callum, speechless, steps in, shuts the door and follows Jenny, leaving little glistening pools of water behind him with every step.

Telescope

JENNY'S ROOM HAS transformed, and Callum gives a gasp of surprise as he squelches over the threshold. As well as the desk and the bed he'd seen the night before, there are now two bookcases, neatly filled with a dazzling assortment of books of every size, shape and subject. Enid Blyton jostles with Umberto Eco, stacks of *National Geographic*s coorie in next to *Ripley's Believe It Or Not* and a boxed set of *His Dark Materials* holds up a teetering family of well-thumbed *Dork Diaries*. Sitting on top of the bookcase is a pair of bongo drums and a tambourine with streaming, colourful ribbons tied to it. The walls are draped with bits of floaty fabric giving the impression of a desert nomad's tent, and a glowing stick of incense fills the room with an exotic scent. A pot of flowering lavender on the desk is adding to this, and Callum takes a moment to catch his breath.

The only box still visible is a wooden case, open on the floor, and Jenny has settled herself on a beanbag in front of it. It contains an intriguing collection of metal tubes, dials and mirrors, and she is gazing at it in confused befuddlement.

"Do you know anything about telescopes?" she asks Callum, adding, "Oh. Do you need a towel?" when she notices the state he's in.

"I'm fine," says Callum, a claim only slightly undermined by the riotous, snottery sneeze which follows.

"No, you ain't," Jenny laughs, and the next few minutes are filled with her hanging Callum's coat in front of the radiator and blasting him with a hair dryer while laughing at his feeble protestations. This noisy stooshie finally done with, Callum sits, red-cheeked and hedgehog-haired, at Jenny's desk while she resumes her position on the beanbag.

"Now then. Telescopes." She lifts a couple of the metal tubes out of the box and tries vaguely to fit them together. "I got this off my next-door-but-one neighbour as a goodbye present, but the instructions are in Polish!"

"Right..." says Callum. "Umm... Why did he give you a telescope?"

"*She,*" Jenny corrects him. "Our house had a little extension out the back, and I liked lying on the flat roof looking at the stars. I suppose she saw me doing that. Not that you could see many stars where we lived. Lucky if you could even see the moon, actually."

She looks up at Callum. "You gonna help me here, or what?"

"Aye, sure," says Callum, ignoring Jenny's whispered, "*Ock aye, the noo!*" and settling down next to her. "Where did you say you were from, again?"

"Chatham."

Callum nods and says, "Oh, yeah. Where's that?"

Jenny rolls her eyes. "It's in Kent, innit?"

"Right. Um..."

Jenny cackles. "You're gonna ask where Kent is now, intcha? You're a proper man of the world, you are!"

It takes Callum a couple of seconds to decide whether this is insulting or funny before concluding it's probably both and giving a weary laugh. "Yeah, well," he says, "I know Skerrils better than anyone! Anyway, let's have a look at this."

They unpack all the parts, discovering that the box has a false bottom and that a sturdy metallic stand is stowed neatly in the secret compartment. Callum in particular thinks this is extremely cool, and he concentrates on the stand while Jenny footers with the telescope itself.

At last, they have a construction which at least *looks* like a telescope, and they both stand looking at it in quiet satisfaction. Eventually, they fall to discussing what exactly they'll be able to see through it on a sodden, cloudy morning in Skerrils. Jenny casts a critical eye at her little window.

"What's out that way?" she asks.

"On a clear day you'll see the Mount..." Callum begins,

then falls over

as he is suddenly

pummelled

by a welter of images,

a clattering

gaggling

kaleidoscope

of rock
and leaf
and storm cloud
and animal
and Skerrils
upon Skerrils
upon Skerrils.

He opens his mouth in a silent scream, clamps his eyes shut, covers his ears and curls into a ball on the floor. Behind it all is the sense of an old, *old* man, an ungraspable figure entwined in the chaos, and Callum wants to reach out and grab him and push him away all at the same time.

Something happened! Something happened with the Mountain and I can't, CAN'T remember...

"Jeez!" yelps Jenny, dropping to her knees at Callum's side. "Mum! MUM!" she yells, and in seconds, her mum is in the room, oh-my-goodnessing and shaking Callum's shoulders.

"What happened?" she demands.

"I don't know!" cries Jenny. "He's taking a fit or something!"

All this time Callum is rolling on the floor, afraid to open his eyes because when he does, the whole room seems to be leering at him, the little potted lavender waving frantically at him and shouting his name.

"STOP IT!" he yells, making Jenny and her mum leap back in alarm, and instantly everything is normal again.

He sits up. He blinks. The room is just a room.

"Are you all right, love?" asks Jenny's mum. "Can I get you a glass of water or anything?"

Callum gets to his feet, wobbly and embarrassed.

"Um, no thanks, I'm fine. Actually...I couldn't have a cup of tea, could I? Milk and three sugars?"

"'Course you can, darling. Coming right up. I expect it's all a bit much, being in here without your granddad, isn't it?"

Well, that's as good as any explanation Callum can give, so he offers a weak smile and a nod. Jenny's mum gives his shoulder a squeeze and bustles downstairs, Jenny shouting, "I'll have one too, ta!" at her departing back. She turns to Callum.

"That was weird. You're a bit weird, Callum. Anyone ever tell you that?"

After the tea, and lengthy reassurances that he really is fine, Callum decides he'd probably better get home.

"Well, hang on," says Jenny. "Don't you want to test the telescope first? Get ready to explore the cosmos? Or at least make sure we put it together right?"

Callum smiles. "Aye, sure." They tilt it so that it's aiming out the window, where the rain has at last washed itself out but the sky is still the colour of lead. "Here goes!" He bends over the bit they reckoned was the eyepiece and peers in.

"Ah."

"What?"

31

"I don't think we got it quite right."
"Why, what can you see?"
Callum stands up and laughs.
"All I can see is my own eye looking back at me!"

News

THE DAYS OF wall-to-wall fun and adventure in Skerrils seem like a distant country to Callum as he sits, bored witless, in front of Sunday-afternoon telly with his mum the next day. He hasn't said anything to her about the bizarre turn he took at Jenny's house. In fact, he wouldn't have even mentioned Jenny to her at all, but Skerrils being the place it is, Mum already knew he'd been round there by the time she and Dad got home from the garden centre.

Conversations with Mum about girls always seem terribly loaded these days, like she's hoping for some big revelation, and she often puts on a serious *you know you can tell me anything* face when the subject comes up. This, of course, makes Callum want to run a mile. Fortunately this time, the fact of Jenny being a girl seems to have been overruled by the fact that Callum has been in Papa's old house, so they can focus on that and leave Jenny in the background. Or at least, they *could*.

Now that Callum has assured her that it was okay, and that it doesn't even feel like Papa's house without him in it, he can sense her curiosity growing. She keeps throwing him meaningful glances during the ad-breaks, trying to start conversations with a long "Sooooo..." but so far he's managed to head her off by offering cups of tea, going to the bathroom or telling her he's heard her PingMe alert braying from the corridor. (Mum has chosen a donkey as her signature sound. When asked why, she responds, "Because I like their big furry faces.") He's running out of excuses now, and his only options are to leave the house entirely or to get the conversation over with. Mum's gearing up for it, so he heaves a sigh and prepares himself.

"Soooo..." she begins.

"Yes?"

"Jenny, eh?"

"What about her?"

"Is she, you know... Is she nice?"

Callum slumps back on the couch, aware that there's no answer that will satisfy her, and anyway he has no idea whether Jenny is nice or not. I mean, she *seems* friendly, and she makes him laugh, but she does that whole *och aye the noo* stuff, and she speaks a bit funny, and it looks as if she reads strange books and things and, well, he supposes he'd like to get to know her better, but she already thinks he's weird and...

And then, glory hallelujah, the doorbell goes.

"I'll get it!" Callum almost shrieks, leaping to his feet and dashing from the room. To his surprise and delight it's Steven. Wonderful, splendid, good old Steven!

"Get a phone," says Steven grumpily. "I can't believe I have to come all the way round here when I want to speak to you!"

On a normal day, this might have started a cheerful argument—Callum might have pointed out that Steven only lives two streets away, for example—but he's so relieved at the distraction that he just nods.

"I'm away out, Mum!" he shouts over his shoulder, grabbing his coat and slamming the door behind him.

It's a grim, grey day, the clouds so low you could reach up and rinse your fingers in them, but Callum's just happy to be outside. Steven's mood matches the weather, though, and he's still grumbling about Callum's stone-age attitude to technology.

"I mean, seriously, Callum," he says, "how d'ye even know what's going on without a phone? Anything could be happening in the world and you wouldnae have a clue!"

"Well," says Callum, "I can watch the news if I want to. Which I don't, really. Anyway, what do you mean, 'Anything could be happening'? We live in Skerrils, for goodness' sake. Nothing ever happens, and if it did, some wifie on the corner would tell you about it faster than you could get your precious phone out your pooch!" He expects at least a smile from Steven, but his pal is just staring at him, open-mouthed. They've wandered more or less in the direction of the shore wall, and the sound of heaving waves on the shingle beyond is filling the air with a chilly restlessness.

"I *knew* it!" cries Steven. "You haven't heard, have you?"

"Heard what?"

"Not even about the BT engineers?"

"Steven," says Callum, exasperated, "I've been inside watching *Antiques Roadshow* with my mum. I don't exactly have my finger on the pulse!"

Steven shakes his head in mock disgust. "See," he says, "this is why you need a bloody phone. Check this out!" He pulls his own phone out of his pocket, gives the screen a couple of swipes and passes it to Callum, who peers at it. The screen is showing the front page of the *Oban Times*, and a report of two missing phone engineers who never came home from working in Skerrils on Friday. There's a grainy picture of the two men, and Callum thinks they *might* be the guys he waved at through the window of the school bus, but he can't be sure.

He passes the phone back to Steven and shrugs. "Okay. But, y'know, it's only been a couple of nights.

They're probably just out on the ran-dan, d'you not think?"

"Fine," says Steven. "What about *this* then?" He's footering with his phone again, and this time when he passes it to Callum, it's showing a shoogly, out-of-focus video. It's hard to make out the details, but the setting looks familiar to Callum.

"Is that the Tinkers' Cave?" he asks.

"Aye! This is Roy McKenzie. He was walking his dog yesterday afternoon. But shoosh—listen!"

The footage bumps and wobbles towards the mouth of the cave and then zooms in, making it even harder to distinguish the blurry images in the mist, but Callum is pretty sure he's looking at a figure lying on the cold, stony ground.

"*Excuse me!*" comes a voice through the speaker. "*Excuse me, are you okay?*"

"That's Roy!" whispers Steven in Callum's lug.

Callum gives an impatient "Wheesht!" and peers at the phone. The figure on the ground does not appear to be moving, and for a horrified moment, Callum thinks he's seeing footage of the discovery of a corpse, but then Roy's voice calls out again, and this time, the figure moves. Slowly, chillingly, like frost spreading up a window pane, the figure rises and turns. Callum's first instinct is sympathy, concern, but even in this poor-quality video he quickly sees that the man on

37

the ground does not require either. The face is cruel, ancient, hard, the eyes dark and piercing.

"Jeez," says Callum. "Him!"

"Aye!" Steven's voice is tight with suppressed excitement. "The Ghost-man himself! Roy says he was just lying there. I'd have legged it, but ye ken Roy. He's no feart!"

Roy's voice now comes from the phone again, asking the old man what he's doing and if he needs any help. Then the only noise coming through the tinny speaker is wind and drizzle, but Callum can see that the old man's lips are moving, his unblinking eyes staring right through the phone directly at him.

"What's he saying?" whispers Callum.

"He's saying he's listening for the pipers in the hill!" says Steven, eyes wide though he's already watched this a dozen times. "I'm telling you, Callum, weird things are afoot in Skerrils. *Very* weird things!"

Drop-In

Now, CALLUM MAY well know Skerrils better than anyone else, just as he told Jenny, but things do change even in tiny West Coast villages, and as he sits at the breakfast table with his mum the next morning, he is puzzling over a brochure she has placed in front of him.

"So," he asks, "what exactly is a youth drop-in?" He feels there must be more to it than the brochure suggests, consisting, as it does, of a photo of a PS3 and another of a ping-pong table.

"Just a place to hang out, I think," says Mum. "I mean, there's not a huge amount for you lot to do in Skerrils, is there?"

Callum feels a strange compulsion to rush to Skerrils' defence, to list the many fabulous adventures he couldn't have had anywhere else, but the sight of yet another grey and colourless day through the kitchen window isn't doing a great deal to inspire him, and instead he says, "Hmmm."

"It's in the old doctor's surgery," Mum continues, "which is great because it's been standing empty since they moved to the new building, and I was just saying to your dad there what a waste of a—"

"Mum," interrupts Callum, "have you heard about that old man hanging about at the Tinkers' Cave?"

Mum gives an involuntary shudder, then forces a smile. "What old man?" she asks, but she asks it in a sort of *let's not talk about this* tone, so Callum drops it.

(This is, after all, how adults have been responding to questions about the old man for the last few months.)

"Oh, never mind," says Callum instead. "What were you saying about the drop-in?"

Mum happily resumes her fascinating account of who exactly did up the old doctor's surgery, how much it probably cost, what the neighbours thought about it and how Donnie, the guy who's running the new drop-in, seems nice even though he's a vegetarian. Callum's attention is beginning to wander till he hears his mum mention something about musical equipment, at which he sits up straight and looks eager.

"Did you say there were instruments there?" he asks.

"Pardon?" Mum seems quite surprised to find anyone was actually listening to her, and she pauses for a second as if she's trying to remember what she was saying. "Oh! Um... Yes, yes, I think so. It was Mary O'Sullivan was telling me about it. You remember Mary—she used to childmind for Jeanette and

Patrick's wee girl, before they got the au pair lassie in from Poland. What was her name...Magda? Maya? Magdalena?"

Urgent though it clearly is that they should both recall the name of Jeanette and Patrick's wee girl's Polish au pair, other matters are driving the thought from Callum's mind. Instruments at the drop-in—and Vicky due back today!

Excusing himself and tidying the plates away, Callum leaves Mum to send a PingMe to Lizzie at the garage (because, being Patrick's second cousin, she'll remember the all-important name) and heads to his room. He finds he's grinning and he's not sure why, but he does know that the presence of new musical instruments will draw Vicky to this drop-in like a wasp to a picnic, and he's determined to be there when she appears. He's also deciding that Jenny would love to meet Vicky and thinking he'll swing by her house on the way past.

So it is that half an hour or so later, he is out on the street, marvelling at just how many different shades of grey he can see and heading in the familiar direction of Gilmartin Street and the cottage down the bottom. There's a tiny, fleeting moment when he realises he is now completely thinking of it as Jenny's house, whereupon a wave of guilt and sadness threatens to skoosh over him. Then he remembers that Papa would

41

be the last person in the world to mind such a thing, to put any faith in sentimentality. In fact, he almost believes he can hear Papa laughing—that old, familiar chuckle, like a pat on the shoulder, and if he didn't know better he'd say he could smell pipe smoke. He closes his eyes, just for a wee minute, before chapping on the door.

Jenny is happy to see him, and soon they're out strolling, collars up against the cold, towards the old doctor's surgery. Gusts of chilly wind ruffle their hair and send flurries of crispy leaves skiting up the street ahead of them. On the whole, it would be a rather miserable scene, but as they approach the drop-in, Callum can hear the first strains of a sound that is at once unmistakable and brand-new—the skirling, leaping, joyful swirl of Vicky in full flow. Suddenly the greys aren't greys but silvers, glinting with a dark, sparkling promise, and Callum forgets ever having thought that Skerrils was dull or miserable.

"That's her!" he shouts, grabbing Jenny's hand and hurrying forward. Jenny follows in baffled amusement as Callum pulls her on. "That's definitely Vicky!" He's laughing as he realises that it's an electric guitar she's wielding, a new instrument for her as far as he knows but one which she can evidently set in singing, chiming motion as easily as if she'd been born with it in her hands. The music gusts and swirls down the road towards them, drawing Callum on and casting the drifting leaves as effortless, joyful dancers.

And suddenly, just as he had in Jenny's room two days before, Callum finds himself utterly overwhelmed and unravelled. Too fast for his mind to keep up, he is suddenly one of them, a dry, skeletal leaf, blown and tummelled on the waves of Vicky's melody. One of thousands, part of a shapeless, shifting mass, part of a thing which once was *green*, a thing of green, time is an endless twisting melody and he is a lost and helpless remnant of Things-of—

"*Callum!*"

"Ahhhhh!"

Jenny's voice has called him back to reality, and he finds he's on his back, sprawled awkwardly on the step of the drop-in, the scream still hoarse in his throat. There are figures standing around him, and Jenny is kneeling by his side, still holding his hand.

Oh, but he was *so close*! So close to knowing, to *remembering*. His eyes fill with frustrated tears that spill down his cheeks, and he blinks, bumbaiselt, the world a swirling blur and the music still ringing in his ears.

Except the music *can't* still be ringing in his ears because as his vision clears, he sees that one of the figures gazing down on him with an inscrutable smile and shaking her head gently is his dear old chum

Vicky. Her arms are folded and her head is tilted, still the image of an alert, inquisitive robin, and Callum feels a bubble of relief and love burst out of him as a slightly manic laugh. She joins in with a brief laugh of her own.

"Well," she says, "nice to see you're as sane as ever!" Then, nodding to Jenny and taking Callum's other hand, she pulls him to his feet. His legs are shoogly and he's almost down on his dowp again, but Vicky grabs him, partly for support and partly for a half-embarrassed hug, which Callum returns with helpless gratitude. Vicky is home. Skerrils can be Skerrils again.

Tree

WHATEVER CALLUM'S MUM might have thought of the refurbishment of the doctor's surgery, it's quickly plain that the new drop-in is a bit of a work in progress. 'Wet Paint' signs are dotted around the various rooms, and while there is indeed a PS3, it is sitting in a tangle of disconnected cables in a corner with no sign of a telly to hook it up to. None of this is important to Callum, of course, who is happily allowing Vicky to lead him and Jenny into the music room. This is up a narrow flight of stairs, whose new blue carpet is filling the building with a synthetic smell, past a little common room where three or four listless teenagers are sprawled across cushions and old armchairs, and through a door that is still marked 'Dr. Harrison'. The last time Callum was in here it was to get his tonsils looked at, and it seems as if this room, at least, is going to be more fun in its new incarnation. There are some African drums in one corner, a dusty turntable on an old desk, and four or five guitars in various states of decay and a mandolin missing half its strings piled under the open window.

"Have a seat," says Vicky, indicating a narrow, two-seater sofa, which looks very much as if it may have been salvaged from a skip in the recent past. Callum and Jenny plonk themselves down, Callum a little self-conscious about just how very snug the fit is, but Jenny apparently unconcerned that Callum is all but sitting on her lap.

Callum feels he'd better make some introductions as Vicky settles herself on a stool next to the still-buzzing electric guitar amp. "This is Jenny," he says. "She's moved into Papa's house."

"All right?" Jenny smiles. "You're Vicky, right? He in't shut up about you all morning! Cool playing, by the way," she adds, pointing at the guitar. It's propped against a wall decorated with an amateurish mural of a tree, its bare, spreading branches criss-crossing a rust-coloured backdrop.

Vicky gives a wee nod. "Hi Jenny," she says. "Where are you from, then?"

They spend the next five minutes or so getting to know each other, and Callum is quietly pleased to see them getting along at once. Jenny is explaining that Callum likes to pop round to her house in order to have violent and alarming fits on her bedroom floor, and Vicky is reassuring her that in fact Callum has a history of startling everyone with his mild insanity.

"So it's not just for my benefit, no?" asks Jenny, nudging Callum gently in the ribs.

"I can actually hear you both, you know," says Callum, with an indignation that is only half put-on. "Anyway, Vicky, *you* can talk. I'm not the one who wanders off halfway through a conversation because I've got distracted by the tunes playing in my head."

If Vicky had been minded to object to this characterisation, her argument would have been undermined by the fact that she picked up the mandolin while Callum was talking and is now playing a jaunty little slip-jig on it, undeterred by the missing strings. She seems to have briefly forgotten that anyone else is in the room. Callum opens his mouth to point this out, but then just laughs and rolls his eyes at Jenny. If he's expecting an ally there, though, he's disappointed. Jenny is nodding in time to the jig with an appreciative smile on her face, and rather than catching Callum's eye, she gets to her feet and makes her way to the African drums. She gives each an experimental tap, picks the one she likes the best and settles on the floor with it, beating a simple but effective accompaniment to the jig.

"Oh, god, not another one!" cries Callum, but he can't deny the music sounds great. Realising that neither of the girls need him to officiate their friendship, he settles back into the couch in resignation and lets himself enjoy the performance. The jig bounces around like a wagtail in flight, and it lifts Callum from the moment, filling his mind with thoughts of summer, carefree days in the untrammelled past, friendships, forests, freedom.

And then his attention is caught by something strange.

"Here," he says, "did that painting have leaves when we came in?" The tree mural, which he'd only glanced at on entering, looks a lot more artistic than he'd first thought. There are fine details in the bark, and each branch bears verdant, green buds.

Jenny and Vicky play on, apparently not having heard Callum, and he gets up to examine the painting more closely. The buds really are incredibly well painted; there's a luminosity to them, as if sunlight is shining through them. They could almost be growing, spreading and covering the bare winter branches in a haze of living colour.

The music darts and skips off the walls, Jenny's drumming becoming more complex, syncopated and insistent, Vicky's mandolin passing through light and shade like a cool, clear burn coursing down a heathered hillside.

The leaves *are* growing. Before Callum's fascinated eyes, they unfurl and stretch, pulsing with the hopeful beat of new life. The rust-coloured wall has dropped away as the tree, giant now, and ancient, stretches high above and around him, and its new leaves hush and whisper in the music's swirling breeze. Small birds dart and chatter in its upper branches, and a carpet of cool, soft moss rolls out around its gnarled and twisting roots. Speechless, Callum settles on the welcoming green, not knowing where to look; every aspect offers fresh wonders. There's a red squirrel up there, circling the branches with gravity-defying ease, and down here in the moss, there is the secretive bustle of beetles, slaters and silk-spinning spiders. Ivy twines up the oak tree's giant trunk, and ferns sprout from nooks and hollows in the tangle of broad, strong boughs.

"I... I..."

Callum is at a loss for words. This is at once so completely bewildering, but also so totally familiar, that he feels himself adrift in the thrumming, tangling green.

Four figures stand around him. They have sprung from the tree just as the leaves and creatures have, though Callum knows they have been here all along. He can no longer see or hear Vicky and Jenny, but he feels them near him and is reassured. The figures are small, smaller than children: their eyes are level with Callum's own, though he is seated on the mossy ground. They could almost be picture-book elves or fairies, but they are looking at Callum with such settled power that they seem very distant from children's stories. As he returns their gaze, they too appear to grow, as if they are drawing power from his attention, and they shift and shimmer before his eyes. He has the strangest feeling that as they grow, he is getting younger or at least shedding the cares and troubles of the last few months.

"I know you," says Callum. "I know all of you! You're…" But before he can say their names, he is frozen by a fell wind and an unchancy presence on the edge of sight. Looking around for a clue, Callum is startled to see the thick, green canopy above him darken and crisp, and to hear the soft reeshling harden to a rattling hiss. He sees a leaf, now brown and lifeless, detach from its branch and fall to the ground. Then another, and another, till the air around him is filled with dry, falling leaves and the tree itself fades into grey.

The four figures are engulfed, and they cry out words in some forgotten tongue, but Callum thinks he hears his name amongst them. He can't focus on this for long, however, because the dark, looming presence is now pressing in upon them, and he can almost make it out—an old man, a cold, old man, growing closer as the tree wilts, as the figures diminish, as the cares pile back on Callum's aching shoulders and the wide, welcoming distance turns back into a bare, blank wall.

The music has stopped. Jenny and Vicky are looking at him expectantly, as if he has just spoken and they didn't quite catch him. Totally disorientated, he gets to his feet, his heart pounding and his hands a-tremble.

Ringing in his ears is the cold clatter of winter wind, and a chorus of desperate voices crying, *"Cùm air chuimhne!*

"Remember!"

Reunion 1

"LOOK," SAYS CALLUM, "I'm not going crazy."

It's later the same day and there's a small gathering in the steamy interior of Rico's café, a well-loved but rather shabby wee establishment on the sea front. Jenny has had to go home to help her mum unpack, but Vicky is still with Callum, and they've been joined by Steven. To everyone's surprise, Craig has also deigned to come out, so for the first time in living memory the four friends are together. To say it's just like the old days would be a bit of a stretch: for one thing, Steven seems more interested in Helen, the lass who's clearing the tables, than in his old chums; for another, Craig has a couple of hangers-on. Two of the tough nuts from school have come through from Oban for the day and are sitting impatiently at their own table, glowering out the foggy window and making it clear that they didn't come all this way for this. Craig's attention is continuously being drawn to his phone, which chimes and beeps with the full repertoire of PingMe irritants, but to be honest, he was always a bit like that.

"Yeah, you're not *going* crazy," he mutters, swiping idly at his phone screen, "in the same way that I'm not *going* to Skerrils." Callum and the others look at him blankly. He looks up. "I mean," he says, "I don't need to go there because I'm there already, see? You've been crazy for years, mate."

"Shut up, Craig," says Vicky. "Go on, Callum."

"Well," he says, "I know what it must look like, honestly. If I saw one of you thrashing around on the ground, I'd probably call a doctor."

"Wait till you see who I'm thrashing around with first, please," says Steven, giving Helen the waitress a lurid wink.

She cuffs him on the back of the head as she passes, saying, "Any more of that and I'll tell your mammy, ye cheeky wee git."

"Shut up, Steven." Vicky is impatient. "So, what's going on, then?"

Callum sighs.

"I've honestly no idea. I mean, it's like I keep getting interrupted—" At this point, Craig's phone emits a resounding belch, which draws a cackle from the two Oban lads at the window. Vicky wipes the grin from Craig's face by leaning over the table and plucking the phone from his hand, turning it off and slipping it into her pocket.

"Oi!" cries Craig, making as if to stand up until he sees the look in Vicky's eyes. He sits down and finally turns his attention to Callum. "Sorry," he mumbles, and Callum tries again.

"Everything's just going along as usual, and then there's just this big, pressing *weight,* you know, like a massive load of memories that are desperate to get out. I can't really explain it, but it feels like something, or some*one*, is trying to get my attention. It's like... It's like they're trying to *wake me up.*"

"You know what I think?" says Steven. Vicky tuts in exasperation, evidently not much interested in what Steven might think, but he goes on undeterred. "I think you're trying to look interesting for that Jenny lass."

Callum feels his cheeks go red. Steven is delighted.

"Ah, see! I kent it! Ye've got a massive riddy, mate!"

"I'm not!" Callum protests, but Steven is placatory.

"Hey, no, don't worry about it, Callum. I'm no slagging ye aff, mate, it's a good play. *Man of mystery* kind of thing, aye? I was wondering when ye'd start paying attention to the important things in life. She looks like the type who'd be into that sort of thing, I reckon."

Craig gives a snort.

"Steven," says Vicky, "if you don't shut up, I will punch you hard in the face."

Callum laughs. "Ach, look, I know it doesn't make much sense, believe me. It would be much easier if I was just having a fit or something. But, I mean, it's so *real*, the place I'm going, it's so solid..." He trails off, shrugs. "Maybe it's pointless trying to explain."

All three of his friends are, at last, paying attention, though none of them are any the wiser yet.

"Okay," says Craig, properly engaging for the first time, "but what's it got to do with us? I mean, no offence, it's nice to see you all and stuff, but we're not wee kids anymore and I've got visitors today."

This time, it's Steven who's exasperated.

"What, Tweedle-Dee and Tweedle-Dum over there? Jeezo, Craig, ye ken who yer pals are, don't ye?"

"No, I mean... Look, if there's anything I can actually do, then fine, happy to help. But seriously, Callum, does any of this have anything to do with me?"

Callum looks miserable. At this point, Helen arrives with the four hot chocolates they've ordered, and there's a lull in the conversation as they all tuck in, Callum taking a moment to add three sugar cubes to the already sickly brew before taking a deep slurp.

Slightly energised, and now sporting a fetching chocolate moustache, he makes a final attempt to explain himself.

"You're right, Craig, I know it's a bit weird us all hanging out and everything. But the thing is...

The thing is, it feels as if this all has something to do with that summer. It's that same feeling, you know, the feeling that we're...we're *missing* something, something really obvious, something massive that we should all just, like, *know.* And it's driving me *round the bend*!"

There's a nervous silence, and Callum's friends exchange uncomfortable glances. It's this subject more than any other that has seen the once inseparable friends grow ever more distant.

Two summers before, for a strange and fleeting moment, quiet little Skerrils had felt like a place where huge, important things had happened, and it was true, all four friends had felt it. Not only Callum, Craig, Steven and Vicky, but the *whole town*—everyone— had suddenly felt closer, more aware, a part of some huge and majestic whole. And Callum, somehow, had been at the very centre of it.

But that summer had ended. The three boys had all moved up to the big school, Vicky had disappeared up north, the town had carried on, people came and went, and whatever strange, bright magic had illuminated their lives seemed, to everyone but Callum, to have dissipated like the light of a blazing sunset, too precious and fragile to be held for long.

Callum looks at the three faces around him, and he feels it happening again. He's about to lose them. There's sympathy in their eyes that he doesn't want.

He doesn't *want* them to feel sorry for him; he just wants them to *remember*.

"Callum," says Vicky. There's a gentleness in her voice that makes him want to both weep and scream, and he knows what's coming—knows, but doesn't want to hear it. "Callum, are you sure this isn't just about you losing your Papa? Because, you know, we all miss him, but—"

"NO!" yells Callum, slamming his fist on the table and making the sugar cubes dance in their silver bowl. Every conversation in the wee café stops suddenly, and every eye turns on Callum. He shoves his chair back with a noisy *screech* and jumps to his feet. "I *knew* you were going to say that, but it's *not that*! God's sake, I'm not a toddler! I *know* people die!" His heart is pounding now, and he's struggling to catch his breath. "It was the *Mountain*, for goodness' sake! It was the *Mountain*, and you all know it was!"

Embarrassed diners turn back to their food and drink, and the low hubbub of café talk slowly rises again. Callum feels stranded, standing like a stookie, his friends looking at him as if they're trying to keep the worry from their faces.

Steven attempts a joke. "What mountain?" he says, pointing to the view out the back window. On a clear day, this offers a vista of craggy majesty, the heather-bound foothills marching up to the Mountain's distant, rocky ridge, silver burns and white-foamed waterfalls glinting from the hazy distance. Today, there is nothing to see but grey.

Callum clasps his head in his hands and grits his teeth, trying not to look too much like the lunatic he knows they all believe him to be. "It's not funny!" he wails. "I don't understand why no-one will talk about it! How can everyone know something but refuse to talk about it? It's like... It's like..."

And then it strikes him. "It's like the Ghost-man!" he cries. "No-one'll talk about him, will they? No adults, anyway. Just like they won't talk about that summer, about the Mountain!

"It's something to do with *him*! Everything was fine until *he* came along! He's a threat, he's threatening... He's threatening Things-of... Things-of... *Aaaaach*!" The words won't come, his head feels as full of grey mist as the sky outside, and he grabs his jacket from the back of his chair in frustration.

"Look," he says, finally bringing his voice back under control, "I *know* it's something to do with that old man. And if you won't help me find out what, I'll find someone who will!"

And with that, he turns and stalks out of the café, leaving his friends to finish their hot chocolates in unhappy confusion.

Pibroch

Two hours later, Callum has found his accomplice.

Lucky Jenny, a new face in town, finding her feet after big upheavals in her own life. Let's spare a thought for her, because resilient and savvy as she is, there isn't much in her experience to prepare her for the manic attention of a peculiar boy. When, a couple of hours ago, Callum had come clattering at the front door and insisting that she join him on a walk up to the Tinkers' Cave, Jenny was in the middle of writing an email to her cousin back in Chatham, not exactly sure what to tell her about Skerrils. 'Not much to do' was the phrase she had just typed, but Callum's arrival seems to contradict that. There *are* things to do. They're just strange and apparently pointless things.

Jenny's taken a liking to Callum, of course, and perhaps she feels a little responsible for his well-being since she's moved into a house that means a lot to him. He is also making what might be a slightly boring place quite a lot more interesting than she'd expected. So she hasn't needed a great deal of persuading to join him, and here they are, hunkered down after a long walk and waiting for she knows not what.

A light smir of rain has begun to make itself known, and Jenny shivers in the heather. Callum beside her seems not to mind—doesn't even slap at the midges which tickle and crawl across his skin. His gaze is focused on the cave mouth about a hundred yards away, and nothing's going to distract him.

"I'm cold!" Jenny whispers. "How much longer?"

"Wheesht!" Callum doesn't even glance at her.

The smir becomes a drizzle until rivulets begin to run from Jenny's hair into her eyes. At least the midges are away, but that's little comfort: sharp heather shoots press through her purple cagoule and she's sure every tic from miles around must be marching towards her for a nibble.

"Callum, he's not coming!"

"Will you shut up? I'm telling you, he'll be here!"

Jenny sighs. To be absolutely honest, she'd half-thought Callum's stories of the strange old man were a subterfuge, an excuse to get her alone. She'd even wondered if something a wee bit more romantic than staking out a miserable cave mouth was on his mind and that, just maybe, a tumble in the heather might be fun.

Well, this isn't fun, and she's coming to the disappointing conclusion that Callum, weird as he is, isn't much fun either.

"Right," she begins, "that's it, I'm—" A sharp dig in the ribs silences her as Callum points excitedly at the gravel path.

"Look!" he hisses. "There!"

It takes Jenny a minute to clear her vision of rain, but sure enough, slow and steady up the path, comes a hunchbacked old figure swaddled in odd, grey clothes. The old man looks as if every step is tortuous, an agony. The gnarled stick in his hand barely keeps him upright. Instantly, the chill of the rain is intensified, and Jenny starts to shiver.

So there *is* an old man, and there is certainly something very odd about him. Unsettling, even. Yet Jenny is mesmerised by his slow, relentless progress, and she begins to feel anxious, agoraphobic, wet and exposed and a long way from home. She tries to flatten herself against the wild hillside and shuffles a little closer to Callum, for all the comfort he offers.

When at last the ancient figure reaches the cave mouth, he lays his stick on the ground and settles painfully down beside it. Jenny shudders. The ground is soaking by now. The old guy will catch pneumonia! Slowly as a wilting flower the man lies down, pressing his ear to the stony earth.

"What the bloody hell is he doing?" Jenny hisses.

"I told you," says Callum, unable to hide his delight. "He's listening for the pibroch! He wants to hear the pipers in the hill!"

The story of the old man's strange arrival in the village is fairly new to Jenny but she's sort of dismissed it. People don't just show up out of the hills, not anymore, whatever Callum's imagination might be telling him. This is probably just some old guy who's wandered from his family, maybe a little bit senile, poor bloke.

But as she watches him there on the hillside, she can't deny the strange atmosphere he carries. He seems to fit into this bleak, barren landscape a bit too well, like the wind-blasted rocks of the cave mouth and the lifeless, yellow scrub that clings to the hillside. Her scepticism gives way to simple fascination, with perhaps a little twist of fear.

"Is he okay, do you think?"

"He's fine. He does this every day. Isn't it mad?"

Jenny is about to agree when the strangest sensation fills her bones. "Wait," she says.

A keening whine has entered her body.

"Wait," she says again. "I hear them! I can hear the pipes!"

Callum turns to stare at her as she slowly stands, her fear forgotten.

"It's real! You were right!" she cries. "It's... It's *amazing*! Are you hearing this, Callum?"

But all Callum hears is the wind off the hill, the gurgle of water from a hundred swollen burns and sheuchs. He can't know that to Jenny, the moment has become a rising drone, waves of insistent sound arriving from some unthinkably distant age, a beat behind it like the march of a host of grinning skeletons. Her fingers start to tap in time, and her expression evolves from one of baffled, frightened rapture to one of simple terror. A short distance away, the old man has risen to his feet.

"Oh, Callum!" cries Jenny, her face contorting into an expression of dread. "I don't like it! I *don't like it*, Callum!" Her whole body is now in turmoil as the beat and the skirl encircle her sinews, grip her by the nervous system, infiltrate her bones. She wants to cover her ears, but she has no control over her movements and starts to pace awkwardly on the spot, left, right, in time to the clattering rhythm, a clumsy marionette.

Callum seems paralysed, but for him, it's disbelief at his companion's sudden change that has rooted him to the spot. His mouth opens and closes as he tries to frame a question, but the spectacle before him has robbed him of speech.

Jenny, now convinced she is trapped in a living nightmare, is a powerless observer as her body begins to march, squelching over sodden heather towards the yawning cave mouth. Standing there, beckoning and grinning like a demonic doorman, that ghastly old man is controlling the whole terrifying spectacle as a conductor controls an orchestra. His eyes are blazing with a cold light, his face a hungry, spiteful sneer.

Fighting every step, Jenny draws closer and closer as the deafening cacophony resolves itself into a physical, swirling tunnel. The Tinkers' Cave is a portal, irresistible, sucking her in like water down a whirlpool. It's a swirling, slurping tumult of withered branches, brittle bones, stones crumbling to dust and howling down this deafening, ringing hole in the Mountain.

"*Yes,*" says the old man, his whisper somehow cutting through the din as Jenny feels she's following legions of vanished souls, helpless, foolish, powerless people, dancing at the mercy of an unkind power. And Callum, still frozen to the spot some distance away, watches in horror as she turns to him with one last, desperate effort, then tumbles into the cave mouth and is gone. There is no question of following her. The way is closed.

Although he has not heard the music, could not see the sounds, Callum's ears are ringing and his heart is racing like a hare streaking for shelter.

Gone. She is gone.

Everyone is gone.

Callum is alone.

Help

I T'S STILL NOW, can you see? Still and silent. Callum sits crumpled, miserable and defeated on the wet, mournful slopes of the mist-shrouded Mountain. He'd come up here for answers, to unravel the mysteries of the last few days, maybe even the last few years, carrying the foolish notion that those answers might be exciting, enlivening, a grand adventure like he had when he was wee.

But now, with all the answers he never wanted to hear, that damned old man comes, smoothly triumphant, gliding over the heather like a creeping marsh mist. Callum senses his approach but hasn't the energy to look up. He huddles into himself, cursing his foolishness, begging Jenny's forgiveness, heart-sore and stunned at having walked so blindly into peril. A merciless chill rises around him, and he knows the old man is upon him.

"Don't fight it, Callum Maxwell," comes an icy, hissing voice. "Why fight being alone? Because you *are* alone, aren't you? Like everything is alone in the end.

"Don't fight it, child. *Embrace* it. *Be* alone. *Everyone* is alone. There are just those who are too stupid to realise it."

The voice is certain. It is confident and victorious. But however miserable and broken he feels, our Callum is not a lad to simply accept instruction. He can't yet bring himself to look at his antagonist, but he can reach inside himself to gather his defences.

This thing, this man, whatever it is, is *cold*. Not the thrilling chill of a leap into a river, but the cruel, insinuating cold of chances missed and loved ones lost. And Callum knows he needs to find the warmth, to remember *warmth*. Eyes still closed, he tries to ignore the numbness in his fingers, the clinging, clawing October chill. He thinks of his heart, his warm, beating heart, and tries to imagine times when it was full and fiery. In his mind, he scrolls through faces, people who have brought him joy.

At first the list seems long and he feels his strength growing, but then the old man's whispers grow louder. Here's Craig, look, good old Craig, but the voice says *He sees you as a tiresome child!*

Now Steven's face, a surge of joy, then *Ahh, but what use are you to him now? You embarrass him!*

Mum and Dad, safety, comfort—*They never understood, did they? Your secrets, your triumphs, they know nothing of them and care even less!*

Vicky, wrapped in melody, a spring birdsong in human form—*She left, remember? You were not enough for her!*

It is relentless. Callum doesn't want to go deeper, doesn't want to conjure the one face that was *always* there for him, doesn't want to hear what the vicious old voice will have to say about that one. He won't have his memory spoiled, his love questioned, so he forces himself to open his eyes. He is prepared for almost anything—to stare down this cruel spectre, to jump to his feet, demand that Jenny be brought back, be the young hero battling against the odds, however terrified he may be.

But the old man is nowhere to be seen.

What Callum can see, the sight that clatters in upon him, is worse than any strange old man. It's worse because it's not a new sight. It's a sight that has been in front of him for months but one which he has refused to allow in. He has ignored it, put it aside, tried to paint over it with distractions and trivialities. But here it is, in crystal clarity.

It is a world without Papa. A world where Papa is not.

And Callum folds. Crumples.

Slumps to a huddle.

Cries.

But...

As Jenny disappeared through the gateway to the Mountain, and the old man cackled in delight, unseen, unsuspected, something—someone—travelled in the other direction.

As the girl was lost and the world made poorer, another, long, long lost, returned.

And she is here.

And she approaches Callum.

And she touches his shoulder.

"What?! Who...?"

He knows at once it is not the old man. The touch is not cold. It is startling enough to make him leap near clean out of his skin, however, and he's on his feet and backing away, gasping in alarm.

Not cold. *Fizzing.* Strangely familiar. And there she stands.

She is tall and slim and stately, and she has, somehow, put his fear on hold. Whatever power the hideous old man was wielding is suddenly forgotten, uninteresting. She seems ancient yet full of life, almost aglow. Her silver hair flows long and elegant down her back and rises on the wind like the white crests of waves on a spring swell. Although she is looking to a far horizon and not yet at Callum, he can see her eyes are kind and wise but with a flash of mischief at their heart. Her half smile, when she finally turns it on him, says, *Yes, things are hard, but wait awhile, for change is always on the way.* Callum is entranced.

"Who... Who *are* you?" he asks.

She takes a deep breath and spreads her arms, like petals opening to the morning sun. Reaching high, she clasps handfuls of air, and for the first time in weeks there is a break in the clouds, a streak of blue, and the hint of the Mountain's majesty unshrouded. Callum looks up, hearing the far, plaintive cry of a golden eagle, and there it is, silhouetted in the mighty sky. The merry gurgle of burns and streams rises again, where moments before all had been frozen silence.

"Ahh, who are we?" she asks. Her voice has a familiar lilt to it, a taste of islands, of distant salt spray. "We have been gone for a long time, have we not? But you should know us, Callum. We know you!"

This 'we' business, now, that is exactly like... someone... some*thing*...

"We," she continues, then pauses, gives her head a little shake, brings her arms back to her sides. Something of her wild magic recedes, replaced by a shining humanity, leaving Callum with the impression of a morning haar burnt off by the rising sun.

"*I*," she starts again, her ancient face creasing in a warm, simple smile, "I, Callum, am Elsa. I am your grandmother, and I am here to help."

Reunion 2

THERE'S COLOUR ON the mountainside again.
A landscape that has for weeks been as appealing
as a mouldering bath sponge is suddenly revealed as
a mosaic of golds and purples and cinnamons. Also,
maybe because it's been hidden for so long, the open
sky seems a deeper, more livid blue than Callum can
remember seeing, as if it's rolled its shoulders and
taken a long, refreshing breath. Things are moving in
a steady breeze, but the autumn chill no longer seems
a portent of a deadly winter. Instead, it is a thrilling
new flavour, and the hillside is alert and ready for it.
It's a time for gathering, for hoarding, for laying in
supplies. The busiest, most urgent time of year in fact,
though Callum has been blind to it till now.

All of this is possible because of the impossible
woman standing by Callum's side. It's as if she's given
permission for the world to wake up from a dim and
misty dream, and Callum feels his bones refilling with
the strength that the old man drained from them.

He stands.

"You can't be," he says simply. "You can't be Elsa. Elsa's been dead for years."

"No, *a ghràidh*, she hasn't. Gone, but not dead. And," she adds, cocking her head as if something has just occurred to her, "not really *gone*, either."

Callum rubs his eyes and gives his head a shoogle. There's no denying it. She's there, as solid and real as the glittering boulders and the bouncing heather.

"So where have you been?" There's nothing accusatory in Callum's question; he's just curious.

Elsa gives him a long look. "I have been here and there," she says. Callum gets the sense that she means more by this than the words suggest, a sense that's only strengthened when she adds, "And so have *you*, Callum."

"I don't understand."

"Good," says Elsa. "I would be worried if you thought you did. Come." She takes his hand in hers, and her clasp is warm and soft and strong. "We will walk awhile."

They walk in silence, leaving the troubling cave far behind. Their path changes from well-worn to non-existent, but Elsa guides Callum effortlessly past sucking bogs and sinkholes, over crumbling rocks, sometimes climbing, sometimes descending. They seem to be tracing a particular pattern on the mountainside, though it's a strange one to Callum.

Usually, his mind would be birling with questions, but right now there is nothing upon him but a grateful peace. When he does speak, it is to make a simple observation, one which has been growing in him as they walk.

"You're beautiful," he says, a little surprised at himself as the words come out.

Elsa smiles at him. "We are, are we not?"

Although it had not been clear that they were heading anywhere specific, when they finally stop, Callum can tell this has been their destination all along. They have made their way to a shining stand of birch trees, the last leaves rustling in the golden wind. Ducking under branches and lowping over stones, they reach a clearing in the middle of the trees and find a deep, dark pool ringed with rough, mossy boulders. The water is disturbed by skiting pond skaters, whirligig beetles and water boatmen, a busy cosmos sending glistening ripples ringing to the shore. Though the water is as dark as well-brewed tea, Callum senses bigger creatures below, biding their time as they prepare to make a meal of the unwitting beasties at the surface. A sparkling, peaty burn flows into one end of the pool in a constant dance of silver bubbles and pulses out again at the other over smooth, slick stones. *Like a heartbeat,* thinks Callum, as he settles next to Elsa on a lichen-crusted rock.

At last, over the hush of leaves and the chuckling water, Elsa speaks.

"You are troubled, *a ghràidh*."

Despite the tranquillity, Callum's birse begins to rise. He turns to glare at her.

"Of *course* I'm troubled," he snaps. "I'm troubled because I've just lost my friend!"

She meets his gaze, those eyes as deep as the pool beside them. "No," she says. "You have just lost your friend because you are troubled. The one who took her *knows* you are troubled, and he wants only to see those troubles grow. If he can turn your friendship into a source of distress then he will be more than satisfied."

Callum opens his mouth to answer but stops, confused. Elsa goes on.

"I know you, Callum. I know you well. You wish to run, to win, to rescue, to solve. You wish to show that you are strong, that you will not be beaten. You want control.

"This is not a *bad* thing. Your Papa was the same, as a boy." She smiles a gentle smile. Whatever protest was rising in Callum, the mention of Papa has silenced it. "There is a time for mastery, Callum, for heroism. But there is also a time for watching, for listening. For preparing."

In the swaying branches of the birches, small birds flit and twitter, busy, oblivious, their bright feathers catching the lowering sunlight.

"So what do I do?" asks Callum. "What do I tell Jenny's mum? *Sorry I lost your daughter. I'm just watching and listening for a way to get her back*?" He regrets his tone instantly, as a flicker of disappointment passes over Elsa's face.

"Ah, Callum," she sighs. "You know better than that. Your friend's mother would not know what you were talking about. She has already forgotten her daughter. And there is a great comfort in forgetting sometimes."

Callum leaps to his feet. He is about to be overwhelmed by a feeling of helplessness, and he cannot—*will* not let that happen.

"No!" he shouts. "There's a way! There's a way to get her back, to get *everyone* back! And... And I don't know exactly *what* I'm going to do, but I'm going to do *something!*"

Elsa rises gracefully and smiles. "Yes," she says, "you are. *We* are. It will be good to do something, I suppose. We will feel as if we are acting. We will feel as if we are solving the problem."

"So we're going back to the cave, then?" Callum's already heading in the direction they had come. Elsa holds up a hand.

"Ah, no," she says. "That is not a good way in. Sometimes the way you begin can colour the whole journey, no matter how good or noble a journey it is. We must find a *different* way. We must not be dragged there by an enemy. We must be *invited* by our friends."

And then the nature of the day begins to shift. Everything suddenly seems more than itself. Callum's gaze drops to the mossy ground, and every tiny green fleck is staring into him with blazing eyes. The moss begins to shimmer, to tumble in upon itself and slowly rise in emerald folds to form a figure of roots and branches and deep, green mischief. Callum jumps back and spins to see the rocks rise wet from the burn and slowly, grindingly, deliberately form themselves into a dark and rugged human form. Next, a commotion in the branches grabs his attention and he turns to see a feathery stramash, as bird after bird comes streaking into view and divebombing into a growing blur of wings and beaks and little claws, swirling, chittering, screeching, and finally resolving into a vibrating, grinning figure who hops down out of the branches, landing lightly on the grass. And last of all, from out of the deep, dark pool, the water swirls and rises with a slurping, sucking, sloosh, emptying the pool and forming a fourth, shimmering figure who, like the others, gazes expectantly at Callum.

Things-of-Green.
Things-of-Stone.
Things-of-Blood.
Things-of-Water.
And Callum, eyes open and memory clear at last, laughs aloud and says, "Oh, yes! Of course! Well, it's about bloody time you all showed up!"

Entrance

AND THIS, DEAR reader, is where things begin to get weird.

The four figures start bouncing and capering around Callum like a pack of puppies who haven't seen their master in days. This is not a particularly good look for ancient beings of unknowable power, but Callum is completely caught up in the excitement and laughs delightedly for the first time in months. Elsa stands patiently by as Things-of-Green and the others shimmer and shape-shift and cackle and spin.

"You remember, Callum Maxwell!" cries Things-of-Blood as he phases from horse to otter to eagle to shrew. "You remember us!"

"I do!" exclaims Callum. "I remember everything!" He is suddenly perfectly aware of his surroundings, from bedrock to soil to branches to sky, thinning clouds revealing ever more of the endless blue and a million million living things just like him, present and aware. How could he have forgotten this? How can Steven and Craig and Vicky, even *Vicky*, have been carrying on for two years as if they didn't know the truth about where they live? They gave this up for something, let go of this sweet knowledge in the name of carrying on, and where has that got them? They barely speak to each other anymore and their lives are a parade of distractions and interruptions and low-level background unhappiness when all of *this* is right *here*, right *now*.

Leaves leap up on a sudden, bracing wind, tossed and woven by Things-of-Green who seems as young as a fresh spring morning. He grabs Callum by the hands and spins him around till he feels like a storm-tossed leaf himself and all his strange fits and starts of the last few days make perfect, hilarious sense.

Much as Callum would like to spend a wee while reacquainting himself with these marvellous, baffling beings, it soon becomes clear this is not the time as Elsa raises one graceful hand, bringing the riotous reunion to a halt.

"Enough," she says. "We have work to do, friends, and this is not the place to do it." She points to the pool, now empty of water and apparently bottomless, a yawning hole leading deep into the Mountain itself.

Things-of-Water is the first to react, shedding all lichtsome playfulness for an air of urgency.

"Indeed," he whispers. "You are required within, Callum Maxwell!" He swirls into cloud form and dives headlong into the dark.

Things-of-Stone follows, tumbling out of sight in a rattle of pebble and scree, while Things-of-Blood takes the form of a giant, tunnelling serpent, writhing and sliding into the Mountain without a backward glance.

Things-of-Green pauses for a moment at Callum's side. "You have changed, young Maxwell," he says, peering at Callum with strange, emerald eyes. "All things change, as the seasons do. If you come with us, you will change further. Is this what you wish?"

As far as Callum recalls, concern for humans was never this creature's strong point so he is taken aback at this peculiar question. But what would it mean to avoid change, after all? It isn't as if he's been living in some sparkling paradise lately and, as Papa used to say, *a change is as good as a rest.*

He smiles, takes a deep breath, and says, "I'm in!"

Things-of-Green's face creases in a mischievous grin. "Indeed you are," he says, then boots Callum firmly in the bahoukie, sending him tumbling down, down into the pitch-darkness.

Callum flails and spins as he falls, yelling extremely rude words at the fluttering green entity which has leapt in behind him, cackling. Callum turns in space, just in time to watch Elsa step effortlessly into the void as the circle of daylight closes above them. And so they fall.

Callum yells and curses till his lungs are empty, draws another breath and carries on yelling and cursing. He is convinced that he's going to be dashed on some rocky outcrop at any second, but as time passes, he realises he is falling through a perfectly smooth tube, a flawless cylinder like a monstrous recreation of Jenny's telescope with Callum the slightest photon refracted through the lens. He has no idea how far he has fallen, only that the last trace of daylight has long since blinked closed behind him and that the air rushing past has grown icy cold and laden with a sharp, mineral tang.

After a time, a new light begins to glow, a phosphorescent green which is emanating from the space around him. As Callum's eyes adjust to this, he becomes aware of the vastness of it all. It is almost too huge to comprehend, too big to really fall *through*, and though the wind is still filling his eyes and ears he feels as if he is suspended in a fathomless emptiness.

He also realises he is not alone. There are bodies tumbling alongside him, some diving past with a *whoosh*, some thrashing and twisting as they fall. Many are screaming, some laughing maniacally, but some are silent and purposeful.

And all of them are Callum.

Scores of Callums, hundreds, perhaps thousands, differing slightly in outfit and age and expression but all unmistakably him. It is too much to take in, and Callum's mind enters a sort of stasis, a quiet numbness as if to say, *We are experiencing some technical problems, but normal service will be resumed as soon as possible.* He feels himself thinning, diminishing, and sees all these countless iterations of himself doing the same. Some are protesting, crying in fear; some are shrieking in wicked triumph in a most un-Callum-like fashion; all of them are dispersing as they fall, like dust on the wind.

Then, sweeping around them like a sheepdog at the heels of a particularly unruly herd, Things-of-Green zooms and tangles, always with one glittering eye on our Callum. Somehow he corrals these twisting, chaotic bodies into one formless mass, with our Callum winding and baffling in the middle, horrified as, one by one, his other selves burst into him, merging and conjoining and ruthlessly dragging him back into himself. His ears are ringing with a relentless scream, which he realises is coming from his own ragged thrapple, and as the last of his other selves assails him with all the welcome gentleness of a dunt in the chops, he lands with a calamitous thud, bone-shaken and unravelled, on a sandy beach.

A silver, sunless sky expands above him, and his jangled senses can just make out his four tormentors and the timeless shimmering presence of Elsa.

She seems to have made the descent as easily as she might have stepped over a narrow burn, and she watches him with laughing, expectant eyes.

"Oh, michty, michty me," he groans, a phrase that Papa reserved for the most trying of times. He sits up gingerly, checking for broken bones and not at all sure that he hasn't found any in amongst the chiming chorus of bumps and aches and confusion. Elsa holds out her hand, and Callum takes it, instantly drawing strength from her warm, sure touch but still shoogly as he rises to his feet.

"What the merry hell was all *that* about?" he asks, his voice barely more than a breathless whisper.

Things-of-Blood dances to his side, in human form but clad in fur and feathers and radiating a pulsing, living mischief.

"You are in the Mountain, Callum Maxwell," he says. "The Mountain contains all the Skerrils that ever were, or ever could be. It must also contain all the Callum Maxwells if we are to move forwards!"

Callum sighs. "You know," he says, "this is exactly the sort of nonsense that I haven't missed even a wee bit."

Begin

"SO, WHERE ARE we?"

It's a reasonable question. 'In the Mountain' does not really cut the mustard, because if he were truly inside a mountain, how would he be able to see the sky? Fair enough, the sky he can see is not the normal sky—it's the pinkly shimmering silver of salmon scales, and there's no sun in sight—but it's definitely not just the inside of a mountain. That would be something more like the Trog's cave.

Elsa moves to his side. "We are in a place where questions like that are difficult to answer," she says. "In fact, I shouldn't even say we are 'in a place'. We are, now, *of* a place, rather than in one."

"Right," says Callum. "Well, thanks for clearing that up." He looks around.

They are on a beach; that much is clear. The sea sweeps away from them around a wide, arcing bay, its surface undisturbed by any breath of wind. The sand is soft and pale; colours are hard to be sure of, as if it is lit by moonlight. Off in the distance, there are shapes moving around on the water, but whether they are ships or creatures is impossible to tell. They make Callum slightly nervous, so he turns away to survey the land. Back home, under the influence of Things-of-Green, every square inch of the landscape of Skerrils feels like an old friend, familiar and welcoming, and Callum has the same sense here—that the land is a breathing, feeling thing—but that sense has been derailed, shunted off kilter.

It is at once much more powerful and much less understandable. He feels the way he might if his pals all started talking to him in Swahili, very, very loudly. There is meaning, important meaning, but it is beyond his grasp. It feels like *potential*, like the possibility of things rather than the things themselves.

"Wait a minute," says Callum, "I thought you said this was Skerrils, somehow, but there's nothing here even a wee bit *like* Skerrils." Visually, it is bare and rocky and sloping up to a low, misty pinnacle in the distance. "This is a wasteland!" he says, which brings Things-of-Stone uncomfortably close, a looming presence at his left side. It forms itself out of sand and pebbles and a low-rumbling anger.

"Unmoulded clay, Callum Maxwell," it growls. "This is the Mountain at the end and ready to begin again."

"We are outside of time, *a ghràidh*," says Elsa. "This is the land of the forgotten. It does not travel by seconds and minutes, but from here, you can get to almost anywhere."

"Any*when*," corrects Things-of-Green. "You will always be *here*."

Callum's head is beginning to hurt. "Look," he says, "I came here to find Jenny. Can we just get started?"

"Indeed!" come four fell voices at once, and all of a sudden, Callum is pitched from his feet as the ground beneath him begins to rumble and shake. The air thickens with electricity, the sky darkens, and the distant pinnacle starts to rock and tumble. A jagged crack opens in its side, wider, wider, stretching out across the land like a lightning bolt. From within the crack, Callum sees an ominous red glow, and the ground beneath him grows hot to the touch.

"*Wh...wh...what's g-g-going ON?*" he yells, teeth chattering from the roiling clanjamfry beneath him. He tries to stand but cowps over again as the ground bulges and splits, and great, fiery pits appear around him. Things-of-Stone has grown enormous, exultant, while the others flit and dash about like frightened speugs.

"*Beginning! Beginning! Round we go again!*" they cry, their manic glee infecting Callum with a deep and crackling terror. Acrid smoke is now billowing from the cracks, and above him he sees gouts of molten lava oozing hungrily from the split and sundered landscape.

Gobs of it burst and fizz from the pits around him, and everything is bathed in the hellish red light as the whole unsettled landscape boils over.

"HELP!" shrieks Callum, unable to stand and certain he is about to be swallowed by an advancing surge of lava. Strong hands grasp his shoulders and lift him to his feet, and instantly he is surrounded by a bubble of clear, cool air. He turns to see Elsa, who is surveying the scene with a calm detachment.

"Wheesht, dear heart," she says, "you wanted to get started, and so we are. This is the Mountain's beginning. Born in a storm of fire and destruction, pushed skyward by an unquiet Earth. Impressive, is it not?" All around them is a raging tumult, but Elsa speaks as calmly as if she were telling a soothing bedtime story.

"You mean the Mountain is a *volcano*?" Callum is still yelling, even though it's quiet in the bubble, and Elsa winces at the unnecessary volume. "Sorry," he mumbles, then realises he's got nothing to be sorry about. After all, *he* didn't ask the planet to explode beneath him, but before he can express this, Elsa speaks again.

"At the beginning it is," she says. "At the end, it is the beach you stood upon a moment ago, worn to sand by eons of wind and rain and ice. It is, at the same time, the Mountain that stands, still and eternal, behind your Skerrils. It is every one of these things, Callum."

The eruption is reaching its peak, plumes of smoke and dust and ash spewing into the atmosphere in a glowering column several miles high. The column takes the form of a raging giant, and Callum speechlessly realises it is Things-of-Stone, unleashed and unstoppable, a primordial entity of ground-splitting power. It roars and cackles, flinging sizzling boulders down like asteroids crashing into the sea, reshaping the world. The tumult is terrifying, chaotic, and Callum wants to cover his eyes. Where the burning rubble hits the sea, steam shrieks and hisses and roils and glories, Things-of-Water ecstatic and fizzing. There is the sense that these two entities are fighting, a joyful, cacophonous, catastrophic battle that engulfs sky and sea and sensation. Things-of-Blood and Things-of-Green are nowhere to be seen.

The bubble rises through the raging tumult until Callum, looking down on the scene, sees that everything has shifted. The air has cleared, and the Mountain is still and cool and much, much higher than Callum knows it from his world. That such a thing could rise from the ground seems impossible.

"It's like Mount Everest!" he gasps. From here at the peak, the landscape below them is all but invisible, lost in hazy clouds that hug the foothills, but Callum thinks he can make out the coastline and a shape that could almost be MacArthur's Island. The view is breathtaking but vertiginous, and he decides not to think too closely about just what, if anything, is holding him up here.

Snow begins to swirl and drift around them, small flakes at first, then fat, fluffy clumps, falling and piling and falling and piling, and the Mountain's lofty summit is soon a dazzle of blinding white. Suddenly they are falling with the snow, the mighty peak piercing upwards at them as they tumble. Callum opens his mouth in a silent scream, the whistling air around them robbing him of breath. They batter into the jagged summit, Callum certain of destruction and astonished to find he is unhurt while Elsa smiles placidly as someone who has seen this all before.

They are sliding down the Mountain now, skiting past snow-filled precipices, a vapour trail of sparkling snowflakes flying up behind them. As they slide, the snow becomes ice, becomes a glacier, begins to move along with them, shearing off city-sized chunks of Mountain as it flows. Eons are passing in the blink of an eye and Callum (who hasn't blinked for ten minutes or more) turns to see the lofty peak of moments before gently settle as if the land is letting out a long, cool sigh.

They thunder on, leaving the snowfields and hurtling through burgeoning green, steamy jungles of moss-laden trees, outlandish creatures scattering at their passing. And there are Things-of-Green and Things-of-Blood, flying alongside them outside the bubble, laughing, twirling, merging and splitting and growing and shrinking and flashing a thousand forms a second. At times it seems they are one, then it seems they are splitting, strange forms spinning off them like eddies in a whirlpool only to come to nothing in their wake. Callum shrieks in terrified excitement as their bubble flies through the legs of a dinosaur, some giant sauropod grazing on the trees. It lifts its monstrous neck to bellow at their passing...and is gone.

"I th...th...think I w...w...want to g...g...go *HOME*!" Callum gasps through chattering teeth, and no sooner have the words left his mouth than they are still. He stands, panting, on sun-warmed grass that has been grazed flat by sheep and deer and rabbits. The sudden stillness makes his ears ring, and he feels the way you do when you wake from a dream of falling.

He turns to see the Mountain, just as he knows it but with more trees around its lower slopes. Over there is the monument hill, though no monument stands atop it, and there, down there, is the crooked notch in the coast that is the harbour in Callum's Skerrils. Here, or perhaps now, it shows no signs of development, no walls, no boats; it is wild stone lapped by an untroubled sea.

There is a scattering of crude huts just below them, little more than tents made of wooden poles and animal skins. Some have smoke rising from their peaks, and a low mumble of voices reaches them through the warm, still air.

Callum pats himself down. He is undamaged. He slows his breathing from the mortal terror of a few moments before and shuffles about a bit to reassure himself that the law of gravity is behaving more normally now. Things-of-Green and the others have gone, for the time being, but Elsa stands by him, waiting patiently.

"Right," he says and begins to formulate a clever thought about what this all means when a sharp dig in the ribs makes him yelp. "*Oi!*" he hollers, ready to vent his towering confusion on whatever baffling and mischievous sprite thought that was a funny thing to do.

It's Jenny. Her eyes, wide with giggly panic, are darting from him to Elsa to the oddly tranquil proto-Skerrils around them.

"Anyone want to tell me what the bloody hell is going on?" she asks.

Confrontation

THE DELIGHTED EMBRACE that Callum gives Jenny is so heartfelt and enthusiastic it knocks them both to the ground, and they lie there in the warm grass, shaking with laughter, clinging to each other for dear life. When it seems clear that the ground beneath them is not about to erupt, and that neither of them is going to be spirited away by a devilish old man or flung around through time and space, they roll apart and sit up.

"So, this is completely mental, right?" Jenny says at last. "This is some kind of hallucination or something. I feel like I'm caught inside one of your fits, Callum!"

"What?" says Callum. "Are you telling me that you don't have portals to interdimensional time-slips overseen by insane nature spirits in Chatham or something?"

"Not so much, no," laughs Jenny, then, noticing Elsa, she says, "Oh, hello!"

The old lady dips her head slightly. "*Failte*," she says with a smile. "I am Elsa. I'm glad we found you, Jenny!"

91

Before the introductions can proceed, their attention is drawn to unexpected activity in the settlement below. Figures are emerging from some of the huts, fur-clad, dark people who seem agitated by something. There are men, women and children, more emerging by the minute, talking animatedly in a language Callum has never heard before. It's a scene from an impossibly distant past, mesmerising and disturbing. For a moment, Callum worries that it's him and his friends who have caused the disturbance, but it soon becomes clear they are focused on a stooshie that's going on off to the north, roughly where the road would enter Skerrils if they were looking at it in Callum's day. Following their gaze, Callum sees the source of the alarm.

Two men, wearing high-vis vests and hard hats, are bickering as they take tools out the back of a BT van. How the van got there is anyone's guess: there are no roads here and won't be for several thousand years. It looks as bizarre in this prehistoric setting as a spaceship would in Callum's back garden. This does not seem to have occurred to the two men, who are entirely focused on the task in hand.

"Gonnae pass us that pickaxe, Wullie?" says one.

"Get it yersel', Brian, ye lazy clown," comes the friendly reply. "Ah'm tryin' tae find the shovel!"

They argue for a little longer before finally getting down to work, digging a trench.

"Okay," says Jenny, "if anyone wants to explain what the hell is going on, I'm all ears!"

"The BT men!" says Callum. "They disappeared a day or two ago. Steven was trying to tell me about it, just before he showed me the footage of the old man by the cave!"

"God." Jenny frowns. "D'you think he took them too? What's he playing at?"

A few hundred yards away, the people from the settlement are becoming more and more agitated as the workmen crack on with their job, totally oblivious to anyone and anything else. One old villager, who might be a leader of some kind, is trying to calm his neighbours, but there's a fiery young character from another hut who clearly thinks some violent action is in order. Even without understanding a word of their strange, musical language, Callum and Jenny can both see what's going on.

"There's always one," mutters Jenny as the youngster seems to gain the upper hand. He has shooed the children back into the huts, ducked into his own and reappeared carrying a long, flint-tipped spear. The old man is making calming gestures, but he's mostly being ignored, and all the signs suggest that a rammy is about to ensue. With the angry young man's encouragement, more of the people start retrieving weapons from their huts, and voices rise as the scene changes from one of peace and tranquillity to one of impending violence. A few of the tribe have brought out rattles and drums and they're organising themselves into some sort of battle formation to the accompaniment of these ominous instruments.

Wullie and Brian, the BT engineers, are blissfully unaware of the impending danger, whistling away merrily as they dig. The wee group of hostile villagers are now spreading out as they approach them, spears and axes at the ready and a rising determination showing in their rugged faces. The young man who instigated the attack has smeared some red mud across his cheeks and is looking truly fearsome.

"They'll be killed!" cries Callum. "Is that why the old man brought them here? To be slaughtered by a bunch of stone-age bampots? Come on!" He and Jenny start off towards the workmen at a run, surprised to note that Elsa is already way ahead of them. She almost glides over the landscape, and it's an eerie, oorie sight. Running alongside them, to Callum's surprise, is Things-of-Blood, dressed like the villagers and fizzing with excitement.

"No 'old man' brought them here," he pants as he runs. "It was *us*! We have need of them!" There is no time to consider this baffling revelation as they arrive by the workmen's trench, just ahead of the band of warlike villagers. Callum skids to a stop, kicking up a cloud of stoor, which finally attracts Wullie's attention.

"Awright, son?" he asks, taking off his hard hat and dichting a bit of sweat from his brow. The angry mob have drawn up behind Callum and are worrisomely still, dark eyes sparkling at the workmen in measured fury.

"Awright? *AWRIGHT?*" yelps Callum. "Look!"

Wullie puts his hat back on and scans the scene critically. "Hmmm," he says. He gives Brian a wee nudge. "Here, Bri, check this lot oot!"

His pal looks up and climbs out the ditch with his pickaxe in his hand.

"Aw, aye," he says slowly, looking the villagers up and down. "Lookin' for a stooshie, are ye, lads?"

Jenny splutters with manic laughter. "Are you out of your mind, mate? They're gonna massacre ya!"

As if to prove her right, the angry young villager with the painted face raises his spear in the air and lets out a blood-curdling shriek, which is instantly taken up by the others. Callum is gobsmacked to notice

Things-of-Blood joyfully joining in, shrieking at the top of his voice and shaking his fists in the air.

"*What are you doing?*" yells Callum over the din. "*I thought you said you needed these guys, and your hairy pals here are about to kill them*!" Things-of-Blood tries to ignore this but eventually lowers his hands and scowls at Callum like a petulant child.

"Spoilsport," he mutters.

Wullie and Brian are now standing side by side, their tools raised like clubs.

"Ah'm no huvin' this," says Brian.

"Naw, me neither," says Wullie, then they both bellow, "'MON THEEEENNNN!" and dive forward into the stramash. Callum winces and closes his eyes; he can't bear to see the inevitable slaughter. It's a few seconds before he realises that rather than the sounds of splintering bones and mortal agony, there is only a low mumbling and the sound of semi-embarrassed shuffling. He looks up.

Standing in the middle of the would-be battle, Elsa has her arms raised and a beatific smile on her face. She lays a hand on Wullie's shoulder, and he drops his shovel and gazes at her in rapt adoration. She steers him over to the lead villager, who drops his spear and adopts the doitit grin of a toddler expecting a bit of birthday cake. The two men hug, then turn to the crowd with cheery grins on their faces.

"That'll do, I think, gentlemen," says Elsa, and the whole crowd nods vigorously.

"She's very good, isn't she?" hisses Things-of-Blood into Callum's ear. "A most unusual human altogether!"

The pacified villagers, weapons abandoned in the grass, are now gathered around the BT van, investigating it like curious children. With huge grins, some of them unabashedly tug at Brian's and Wullie's hi-vis jackets and try on the hard hats. Brian has a fur blanket thrown over his shoulders, and Wullie's getting his face playfully daubed with the red mud. The village kids have come running and laughing, and the scene, which looked like imminent bloodshed moments ago, is now more like a cheerful family picnic.

"Nice folk," says Wullie.

"Aye," says Brian.

"Why aren't they interested in us?" asks Jenny, taking Callum by the arm and leading him over to a grassy hummock away from the drama. "I mean, we must look as weird to them as those guys do, mustn't we?"

Callum points at Things-of-Blood, who is still in the thick of things, laughing and joining in with the villagers as if he's one of the gang.

"See him?" he says. "First time me and my friends met him, he made a dog get up on its hind legs and talk to its master. Actually talk, like, not bark or growl or anything. Know how the guy reacted?" Jenny shakes her head. "He didn't. Didn't bat an eye. If there's one thing these creatures teach you," he continues, shaking his head, "it's that folk are very good at not noticing things."

Safe

A SHORT WHILE LATER, the crowd has dispersed, and Wullie and Brian have gone back to doggedly digging their ditch. Callum has been wandering around, making a mental map of where things will be when his Skerrils finally develops.

"Over here," he calls to Jenny and Elsa. "Look! I think this is where Papa's house is!" Jenny raises an eyebrow.

"How can you tell?" she asks, politely refraining from pointing out that it's not Papa's house anymore.

"The view," Callum replies. "Look!"

The others join him and follow his gaze, taking in the sunlit Mountain in all its tree-lined majesty. They're perfectly happy to take Callum's word for it, and anyway it's a pleasant spot with a sun-warmed boulder poking through the grass and heather, so they settle down for a much-needed chat. A scatter of children are playing around the huts off towards the shore, sounding much like children playing in any time or place. Things-of-Blood, Things-of-Green, Things-of-Stone and Things-of-Water are all there, perfectly comfortable and entertaining the children with tricks and transformations. Callum marvels at their easy familiarity with the kids and can't help but wonder why it had to be so complicated for him and his friends to get to know them two years ago. *Changed times, I suppose,* he muses.

"So," Jenny says, "it's lovely to be home and everything, but I am still ever so slightly confused. We're *in* the Mountain, right?"

Elsa smiles. "In a way, yes."

"But *that* IS the Mountain." Jenny looks at Callum for support. "I mean, how can the Mountain be in itself? And what the bleeding heck are *we* all doing here? And *who*," she adds, pointing at four strange figures playing happily with the village children, "are *they?*"

"One thing at a time, child," says Elsa. "You wish to know how the Mountain can be in the Mountain. Tell me, do you ever have dreams at night?"

Jenny is confused. "Yeah, 'course I do."

"And are you in those dreams?"

"Well... Yeah, I suppose so."

"Where, then, do those dreams take place?" Elsa's eyes crease in a smile as she sees Jenny's confusion.

"Wait!" interrupts Callum. "Are you saying we're in the Mountain's dream?"

His grandmother nods. "That is as good a way of thinking of it as any other," she says, "but it is important to know that there is more to a thing, or indeed a person, than its own idea of itself. The Mountain is like you, Callum. It is made of the memories of every living thing that has ventured across it. It is also made of its own memories of those things. We are all in each other, you know. It is a glorious, confusing tangle, to be sure."

"Well, that all makes *perfect* sense," says Jenny, rolling her eyes, "but it don't really explain why *we're* here."

Elsa's face clouds over. "There is...a *force*...who hates these connections. For whom life is nothing but disorder and chaos. The patterns that we weave together—our loves and fears and songs and tales— are nothing more than noise to it. It works ceaselessly to sever our ties, to blind us to our common ground and to quiet the din of connection. *You*, dear heart, were taken by that force. And Callum here," she adds, smiling at her grandson, "Callum is unwilling to accept that fate!

"As to why we are *here*, exactly... Well, these good people," she raises a hand towards the cheery kerfuffle around the huts, "are the first to know the Mountain, and we may strengthen the seam by starting at the beginning. Perhaps this will be a good place to hide awhile."

Both Callum and Jenny allow themselves to be satisfied with this. Whether it's Elsa's soothing voice, or the fact that they're both completely knackered and could do with a rest, they quickly relax into the idea of just stopping for a bit. They lie back on the warm boulder, breathe the heathery air and let the sounds of the sea and the sky wash over them.

"Here," says Jenny after a while, "I'm starving!" She sits up, and her stomach confirms her statement with a musical gurgle. "D'you reckon they've got any food over there?"

Smoke rises lazily from some of the huts, which suggests that they probably do, so the three companions make their way towards the little settlement. Their approach is noticed by some of the children, who come running over and laughingly guide them towards their home. If they *do* notice how oddly Callum and the others are dressed, they're too polite to make a big deal out of it. Some of the smaller ones take their hands the better to pull them to the clearing, and Callum is astonished by how strong they are.

"Jeezo," he gasps as a boy of around eight nearly wrenches his arm out of its socket with an enthusiastic tug.

The wee boy is delighted, and begins chirping, "Jeezo! Jeezo!" to the amusement of his friends. Pretty soon, the chorus has been taken up by about a dozen kids, parroting Callum amid fits of unabashed laughter.

"Well," says Jenny, following behind with a smile, "if you can't beat them... *Jeezo! Jeezo! Jeez*—"

"Aye, aye, aye." says Callum, annoyed but laughing, "*You* try arm-wrestling one of these wee hooligans then! I mean, how come they're so *strong*?"

By now, they have arrived at the little encampment, a wide circle of well-trodden earth with a large fire ablaze in a pit at its centre. A wee pack of scrawny dogs are going about their business in the stoor, scratching fleas and sniffing for scraps.

"Look," says Elsa, gliding up beside him and sweeping a hand towards the children, "they are constantly at work!"

And it's true. Amidst the high spirits and youthful hilarity, the children are as busy as the adults. Some are stripping great sheets of tree bark, pulling off long thin fibres and twisting them into twine. Some are learning to chip stone tools, gathered around the feet of a grizzly old greybeard who corrects their technique with gruff but gentle chiding. Some are weaving baskets from long, springy willow stems, which are just as useful for occasionally flicking passing companions on the bahoukie.

Altogether, it seems to Callum and Jenny as if there are a hundred things going on at once, and yet the atmosphere is one of peace and tranquillity. Amidst it all, Things-of-Green and the others move freely and happily, offering advice, sharing skills and playing with their respective elements as easily as if they were putty. Things-of-Blood, who has been with a small group preparing a fresh deer carcass by the fire, calls Callum over.

"Your friend is hungry," he says and conjures a hunk of roasted meat to pass to Jenny. It smells incredible, and Callum realises that he, too, is famished.

"I'm a vegetarian," mutters Jenny, but she takes the offering and after one tentative nibble begins to devour it gratefully. Things-of-Blood has meat for Callum and Elsa too, and soon they are joined by a group of villagers, work done for the day, and an evening feast ensues. There is gentle conversation, singing and storytelling, and although the language is strange, both Callum and Jenny feel as if they can understand some of the songs and tales.

After a while, a girl, probably roughly Callum's age, comes and settles on the ground beside him, wild-haired and fierce-eyed. She says something to him in her strange tongue, intense and smoky as a peat fire, but of course, all Callum can do is shrug. The girl makes an impatient noise and punches him on the shoulder, hard enough to cowp him on his back.

"Hoi!" he shouts, scrabbling to his feet. In the flickering firelight, the girl also leaps to her feet, which are bare and black on the dusty ground, and squares up to Callum with her chin jutting out. She lifts a hand, and Callum flinches, but she's just pointing over to one of the huts. There is an expectant look in her eyes.

"I... Look, I'm sorry, but I don't understand!" He decides to attempt the friendly approach. He puts a hand on his chest and says, "I'm Callum! CAL-LUM!" He's aware of the eyes of the group upon him, amused and watchful. The girl glowers at him, saying nothing. Callum turns a helpless gaze on Things-of-Green, who is flickering by his side, a green light among the red and orange of the fire. "Ehm...I don't really know what to do here. Do you know her name?"

"I do," replies the grinning figure, "but these ones do not share their names with any but us. Even her family do not know her true name."

Callum is frustrated. "Well, *that* doesn't make any sense! What do they call her, then?"

"Each of these will have many names as they grow," says Things-of-Green with something like affection in his curious eyes. "They earn their titles by the deeds they do."

"Fine," comes Callum's impatient reply. "So what title has *she* earned?"

Things-of-Green thinks for a moment. "It is hard to render in your clumsy tongue, but it would be something like *She Who Devours Boys*!"

The girl now has Callum by the shoulder and is shaking him, pointing again at the hut, and Callum can hear little snotters of suppressed mirth coming from the other children of the village. He turns a panicked gaze to Jenny, who is biting her knuckle to stifle her own laughter, and whispers, "*Help*!"

She gets up, steps over to Callum's side and, solemnly meeting She Who Devours Boys' eyes, places her arm around his shoulder.

"Don't read too much into this," she mutters from the corner of her mouth, "I'm just helping you out, all right?" For one moment, it looks as if the wild girl is considering a challenge, but Jenny meets her stare with unflappable good humour, and at last, with a snort, her stone-age antagonist marches off in disappointment. Callum draws a shuddering sigh of relief and gives Jenny a grateful look.

"Thanks," he says as Jenny squeezes his shoulder and withdraws her arm.

"No worries." She smiles. "I'm just glad that worked. I thought I was gonna have to snog you for a minute there." Then she digs him playfully in the ribs and returns to her spot by the fire.

As stars spread across the endless sky above, it's clear that the evening is over. People are leaving the group in twos and threes, disappearing beneath the skin shelters and coorying in for the night. The young man who had earlier seemed hell-bent on ripping Wullie and Brian to shreds emerges from his hut laden with thick straw mats and heavy furs, which he spreads out for the three companions by the glowing embers of the fire.

As natural as breathing, Callum, Elsa and Jenny settle down under the skinkling sky and drift into perfect sleep to the sound of lapping waves, windblown trees, and the mournful howling of distant wolves, lamenting a future they will never see.

Stone

THE NEXT MORNING, Callum and Jenny are awoken by the cold and they sit up, shivering. Their breath plumes above them, and they pull the furs tightly around their shoulders, blinking in the low dawn light. A couple of dogs who had cooried in next to them leap to their paws and dash off, startled.

"Morning," croaks Callum, his throat dry and his bones aching pleasantly. Jenny wiggles her fingers at him and sneezes. Off in the distance, Wullie and Brian are still doggedly digging their ditch and seem to have been doing so all night, perfectly happily. Whatever it is they're up to, it appears to suit them fine.

Elsa, of course, is already awake and standing some distance away, deep in conversation with Things-of-Stone. If she feels the cold, she doesn't show it, and Callum is struck yet again by her ability to speak to these beings as if she is one of them.

"What's she doing?" asks Jenny, and the two friends decide to go and find out. Keeping a firm hold on their furs, they rise and stagger over to Elsa, who turns to them with a smile.

"You are awake," she says. "That is good. This is a momentous day."

"Yeah, 'good morning' to you too," says Jenny under her breath. Villagers are emerging from their huts, yawning and stretching, many of them ambling down to the shoreline, stripping and lowping into the silvery waves with whoops of glee.

Just the sight of this is making Jenny shiver, but for a fleeting moment, Callum thinks it might be just the thing to wake him up. One sight of She Who Devours Boys heading shoreward is enough to change his mind, however, and instead he asks Elsa, "Why, what happens today?"

"It is the Equinox," she says. "The first since these people settled here. This is a thing which must be marked."

Callum furrows his brow and tries to remember why an Equinox should be important, but Jenny is instantly excited.

"Oh, wow!" she cries. "I know about this! Day and night are equal, right? It's like the turning of the seasons? Me mum took me to Stonehenge one Equinox. It was like a little festival!"

Callum is a little bumbaiselt.

"Right," he says slowly, "but how could these guys know that today is that particular day? I mean, it's not like they have a calendar or anything, is it?"

"That," comes a grinding voice at his side, "is to be rectified today." Things-of-Stone casts a long shadow in the morning sun, adding an eldritch weight to his already unsettling presence. He doesn't stand, he looms, and for Callum he has always been the hardest of the Things to know.

Jenny, who has no history at all with the Spirits of Skerrils, can barely even look at him. Fetching up in a stone-age village is one thing; actually talking to an animated stone is quite another. She's a brave lass, though, so she swallows her unease and asks, "Rectified? How?"

The huge figure beside her turns with a sound like tumbling scree and says, "Come. You will see."

The villagers have finished their dook in the sparkling sea and are gathering in a merry crowd, young and old together, chattering and expectant. At some unseen signal, they all start walking towards the higher ground at the foot of the Mountain, and the excitement levels rise with the golden sun.

Elsa, who is already moving with the crowd, turns and gestures to Callum and Jenny. "You will want to see this," she says, and the two friends look at each other, shrug, grin, and join the crowd. Things-of-Stone stalks forward at their centre, a gravelly crunch in every step, while Things-of-Green and the others bring up the rear. It's becoming clear that each of them has their own groups of devotees, but today is Things-of-Stone's day. What that might mean is anyone's guess. Callum is trying to get his bearings and reckons they're heading roughly towards where the McKenzie farm will be many centuries from now. The strange procession walks together for about twenty minutes, the settlement shrinking away behind them.

"It's all about the tilt of the Earth," Jenny is explaining as they walk, her enthusiasm for astronomy overcoming her lack of enthusiasm for giant, unknowable avatars of Nature. "We orbit at an angle, you see? So for half the year, we're sort of tilted towards the sun and the day is longer than the night, and vice versa, right, and twice a year, when we're right in between the two—"

"Hey," interrupts Callum, who has been listening but is suddenly distracted. "I know this place!"

The group has arrived, and a hush has descended, the villagers forming a rough circle around Things-of-Stone. They're in a deer-grazed clearing with a wide view out across the bay, the Mountain rising mightily behind them. A wooded foothill to the west will one day become the monument hill, which means...

"This is where the Holy Cairn is! Or where it will be, anyway. Wow!" The strangeness of being lost in time suddenly floods over Callum, and he is dumbstruck, here and not here at the same moment.

Elsa steps towards him and, as is becoming her habit, completely fails to make the situation any less weird.

"It will be sooner than you think," she says. "Just watch!"

The villagers have started chanting, a low, rumbling sound from deep in their throats, and one by one they are dropping to their knees in front of Things-of-Stone. The old greybeard who was teaching the children how to knap stone tools the day before begins rhythmically thumping the ground with his open hand, and the others soon join in.

Most of them have closed their eyes, trance-like, and Callum is struck with a memory—something Papa told him once, about Things-of-Green and the others. *You don't need to sacrifice goats to them or anything, but they don't mind if you* do *go in for that sort of thing!* Callum looks at Things-of-Stone, regal and majestic in his circle of admirers, and is reminded of a terrible old god awaiting some sort of offering. And there are no goats around...

Mercifully, it quickly becomes clear that they are not here for some bloody ritual. As the beat of the villagers' hands rises, sounding like a herd of galloping horses, the ground behind them cracks and rends in an ear-splitting rammy. The villagers, bizarrely, don't even react, transported by the drumming and the chanting, but Callum and Jenny lowp in fear, convinced the Mountain is collapsing over them.

The rocks are moving, but it's not a wild landslide.

Mighty chunks of stone, some the size of buses, are shoogling themselves free of the ground and standing, grass and soil cascading from their shoulders as they sprout monolithic legs and step into painful motion. First one, then two, then a dozen, pull themselves upright and march slowly in step towards the circle. They have no faces but seem watchful nonetheless, mindful of Things-of-Stone, who stands, a grim master, sweeping his arms and guiding them into place. The earth shakes at their approach, their massive stone feet crashing in time to the drumming of the people, and Callum and Jenny fall to the ground in consternation.

The shadows of the stones stretch and cross in the sunlight as they shuffle and grind into place, forming a circle around the villagers. The two largest make their way to the far side, between Callum and the sun, and plunge themselves metres deep into the ragged, scrubby ground. At a signal from Things-of-Stone, all the smaller stones do the same, half-burying themselves upright in the morning light. And right where Callum and Jenny are sitting, one tall, flat boulder of sparkling granite begins to keel over. Elsa, who has been watching in calm amusement, grabs them both by their collars and hauls them out of the way just as the stone crashes down flat between two of its fellows.

Callum rolls in the stoor and shrieks, Jenny covers her eyes and swears, and suddenly all is still again. Distant birdsong drifts from the pine woods with the fragrant shush of needles in the wind, and the villagers rise silently to their feet. They pad, barefoot, to where Callum and Jenny are lying, and take turns peering at the stone circle that now occupies the space. Rising perfectly between the two largest stones, the sun is held like a jewel in a crown, and the villagers begin applauding and cheering.

"Equinox," mutters Jenny, struggling to her feet. "There's your calendar, Callum!"

It's the Holy Cairn, holding the year in its grasp as if it's always been there, and will stay there for as long as there is order in the cosmos.

And then, despite a million unanswered questions which swarm around them like a cloud of bothersome midges, Callum, Jenny and Elsa are aware that this is not the time for thoughtful discussion of a marvellous spectacle. The sky has darkened, the villagers are fleeing to their huts, and a chill breeze is rising off the sea.

Things-of-Green, flochtersome as treetops in an autumn storm, has appeared in their midst and is spinning around them in a frantic dance.

"He comes! He comes!" cries the strange figure as Callum and Jenny leap to their feet in dismay, joining Elsa who, for once, looks as apprehensive as they feel. "Stay where you are!"

As he dances, a tangle of brambles and whin spring from the ground around them, blocking their view in a thorny mass. The temperature continues to drop, and Callum's anxious breath now hangs visible in the air.

"We're trapped!" yells Jenny, pacing around the impenetrable, jagged jungle.

"Hush," whispers Elsa urgently. "*Listen*!"

Beyond the dark-green perimeter, a confrontation is taking place. Two voices—Things-of-Green's, high and anxious, and another as cold as the grave.

"They are together!" There is pleading in Things-of-Green's tone. "You have no place here! They are together!" In all of Callum's adventures with this strange being he has never sensed concern or care, and its sudden appearance unnerves him.

The other voice is dry and quiet, but filled with a fell, dark power.

"Bonds are broken," it says. "Your time is almost done!" The sky continues to darken as ominous clouds roll together above them.

Suddenly, a small, brown face emerges from the twisting thorns. It's Things-of-Blood, in the form of a weasel, who hisses urgently at the three huddled figures.

"Get you gone!" he says, and Elsa nods, putting a finger to her lips to quiet the children's frightened questions. She kneels and lays a hand on the ground; a crack appears silently in the grass.

"Come," she whispers.

Callum peers down the new-formed hole, expecting to see a dank, dark cavern, but instead his eyes are met with a sunlit hillside just below them.

"Do we... Do we jump?" he asks, his throat dry with alarm. Elsa merely nods, taking the lead by stepping easily through the gap. Jenny shrugs and follows, but Callum pauses to whisper to Things-of-Blood, "Will Things-of-Green be okay?"

The weasel grins, a reassuring twinkle of mischief in his eyes. "The Other cannot harm us unless he harms you," he says. "Now *jump*!"

Callum does not wait to be told twice. He takes a deep breath and jumps through the hole, landing on Jenny, who is sprawled on the sunlit grass. They both yelp, but in surprise, not hurt, and the hole they have jumped through silently vanishes above them. Elsa is standing, unperturbed but solemn, and she offers them both a hand up.

Callum stands and looks around. They seem to be exactly where they were, the Holy Cairn solid and unyielding before them, but the rough shelters in the distance have been replaced with low, thatched stone buildings. There is now a rough track winding through the settlement to the shore, where a jetty of piled stones extends into the glittering sea. Here they can just make out a man and a child, perhaps father and daughter, casting lines into the sea and blethering happily. Gulls wheel and cry in the blue above them, and Callum can see gannets arrowing into the sea beyond MacArthur's Island. Wordlessly, the three companions make their way towards the oddly tranquil scene. Callum's legs are like jelly, and he daren't ask any questions in case Jenny should hear the tremble in his voice.

As they approach one of the buildings, a huge workhorse stops cropping the grass to look at them, then ambles over with interest. As it clip-clops towards them Elsa produces an apple from out of nowhere, and the giant beast makes straight for her outstretched hand, followed by a cloud of lazy flies at which it flicks with its great black tail.

"Well, this is nice," says Jenny, rolling her eyes. "What's this, then? Iron age? Not much different from your Skerrils, eh, Callum?"

They laugh in relief and flop back onto the grass, exhausted, to the sound of an apple being noisily and gratefully munched by the big, bonny cuddy. Elsa speaks softly in Gaelic and scratches its neck, and for a moment, unexpectedly, everyone is happy.

Wish

WHEN CALLUM AND Jenny are rested, they join Elsa for a stroll through the village. There are a few folk out and about carrying bundles of thatch, driving scrawny-looking sheep in front of them, sitting in the sun mending fishing nets and so on. The sound of hammering comes from one of the larger buildings, and as they approach it they see it's an open-fronted forge with a big, sweaty man inside, hammering a glowing red horseshoe on an anvil before dunking it, hissing, into a barrel of water.

"Here," says Callum as they pass, "I think this bit is still called the Smiddy! It's a B and B now, mind you. Do you think we could pop in and ask for a fry-up?"

"I suppose it's pointless to wonder why no-one's paying any attention to us," asks Jenny. "This is down to your magical pals, is it?"

Elsa nods. "It is partly a glamour, certainly," she says, "but it is also because you are not so strange to them as you imagine. We are all people of this place, after all."

"I'm not," Jenny protests. "I'm from Chatham! We only came up here to get away from me dad!"

"Ah," says Elsa, "but you don't understand. Arriving in a place by choice brings its own, special connection, one which isn't always shared by those who are here by an accident of birth. You have opened your heart to Skerrils, child, or you wouldn't be in this predicament!"

"You ain't really selling it to me," Jenny mutters, but the scene is too fascinating for her gloom to last and they meander on down the track. Some villagers do glance in their direction, and one elderly woman even greets them in Gaelic. This language sounds outlandish to Jenny and she looks to Callum for help.

"I don't speak it," he says to her as Elsa and the old woman blether away, "but my Papa used to."

"It's cool," Jenny says. "It sounds like they're talking in magic spells!"

Callum laughs. "Aye, it always sounds like that, but they're probably just talking about the weather or their bunions or something!"

Overhearing this, Elsa leans over to him and says, "And why, *a ghràidh*, would weather and bunions not be magical?" Then she bursts into musical laughter at his doitit expression, bids the old woman farewell and continues with the children to the shoreline.

On the stone jetty, the man is hauling a glittering mullet thrashing from the sea while his daughter jumps up and down in excitement. With the sounds of the village fading beneath the sound of waves on shingle and the mewling of the gulls, Callum listens to Elsa's strange answers to Jenny's unending string of questions. He's still bewildered by Elsa, glad she is with them and excited to get to know her, but he's far more aware of who she is *not* than of who she is. She clearly knows at least as much as Papa did about the strange, wild magic they are all caught up in, but she is nothing like as comforting a guide.

For example: Jenny has asked her why Things-of-Green protected them back in stone-age Skerrils.

"Why does he care about us?" she asks.

Now Papa, Callum is sure, would have told her how every single part of Nature's tapestry is of colossal importance, would have made her feel valued beyond measure. Elsa's answer is a little different.

"He doesn't," she says. "They don't care. They don't *not* care, they just don't care. It was hatred of The Other that made him act, not love for us, though the outcome was the same and we may be grateful for that."

Callum sees that Jenny is a little crestfallen by this response, and he wishes he could comfort her, but Elsa is continuing.

"I suppose you could say we *interest* them. They find the fact that we plan ahead both baffling and hilarious. You see, Things-of-Green, Things-of-Stone—all of them—they are *unplanned* beings. They just are what they are, and they will continue to be as long as there

121

are connected minds to perceive the world. As long as things keep happening to us, and we keep thinking about and remembering what has happened, it is of no consequence at all to Things-of-Green whether the things that happen are to our liking or not. He will still be, though all our plans should end in disaster. Which, dear heart, they usually do."

It doesn't matter that this explanation agrees completely with everything Callum has learned from his association with the Spirits of Skerrils. Jenny was looking for reassurance, and Elsa hasn't provided any. This makes him angry, for reasons he can't quite put his finger on, and he suddenly can't take another step as he is overwhelmed with sadness that Jenny never got to meet Papa.

Elsa notices he has stopped and pauses herself. She gives him an enquiring look, and there is kindness and patience in her eyes. Callum knows he is being unfair, comparing her, but, well...

And at last he blurts it out.

"I want to see Papa!"

Elsa raises an eyebrow.

"Come on," Callum goes on, "you've told us that everything is here, remembered by the Mountain, haven't you? Well, I don't *care* about the stone age or the iron age or the blinking Plasticine age, I want to see *Papa*! He must be in here!" There's a break in his voice. Humiliated, he sits on the ground and throws pebbles at the sea.

"May we have a moment, dear heart?" Elsa asks Jenny, who nods, smiling, before heading off to the tideline. Elsa sits next to Callum.

"He is *in here*, Callum," she says, placing a warm hand on his heart. Callum sobs, despite himself, tries to turn it into a laugh but fools no-one. Elsa puts her arm around his shoulder, and he crumples into her like a wee bairn.

"Then why can't I *feel* him?" He sniffs. "It's all disappearing! His stories, his voice... Memories are *useless*. I want to be *with* him!"

Elsa sighs, a deep, sad sigh. "Ahh, I have felt the same, *a ghràidh*, more times than you can count. It is some fifteen years since your Papa and I parted, and though we had known of the coming day for decades beforehand it is still an open wound. But he *is* in there, you know," she says, patting Callum's chest again, "like an egg is in a cake. When all is mixed and baked, you cannot remove the egg, but the cake would be no good without it."

Callum thinks about this, feeling bad for having been so pathetic (in front of Jenny), for having thought poorly of Elsa (who is clearly both wise and kind, really), for not being properly astounded at sitting by an iron-age version of his hometown. What she says makes sense, of course. But is it enough?

"OH... MY... GOD!" Jenny's frantic scream cuts through Callum's dwam from down the shore and they are on their feet in an instant, running over shingle to see what has alarmed her.

It doesn't take very long to spot it.

A shimmering, twisting, silvery figure has risen from the waves and is striding up the shore towards them, its expression about as trustworthy as thin ice on a frozen loch. A parade of crabs, lobsters and starfish march up the beach behind it as, in a voice like rain on a tin roof, it says, "I believe *I* can help, Callum Maxwell!"

With that, it grabs Callum by the shoulders, and he feels as if he has been plunged into deep, dark water. The last thing he hears before his senses are completely overcome, is Elsa's frantic cry—

"NO!"

Memories

"A RE YOU OKAY, laddie?"
Callum blinks.

He is on a boat.

He is on a boat in the bay.

He is on a boat, in the bay,
                        with Papa.

And it's incredible! It's like a dream, a hallucination; it's a wish come true! The old man is right there, within touching distance. Those wise, old eyes are looking right at him! Every fibre of Callum's soul wants to leap up and hug his Papa, however unwise that might be in a wee bobbing rowing boat. It doesn't matter. Nothing matters. Everything is right with the universe again!

Except, of course, that it isn't, and this becomes heartbreakingly clear to Callum when he hears himself reply, "I'm fine."

Where the heck did that come from? Why would his mouth imagine that *that* would cover the situation? Not, "Of *course* I'm okay, Papa, *you're* here!" Not, "You have no idea how much I've missed you!"

Not, "Oh, thank *goodness* you're back! We're in the middle of the craziest adventure!"

Just, "I'm fine." That's when Callum becomes aware of the way he is sitting. His arms are folded, his shoulders hunched, and he is about as turned away from Papa as it is possible to be in the confines of the wee boat.

"Would you like another wee shottie at casting off?" asks Papa.

Of course! Of course I would like another wee shottie, dear, dear Papa!

"No. Thanks." Callum's answer is petulant, ungrateful, and he hears it in frantic disbelief. The worst of it, the dirk to the heart, is the fleeting look of hurt that passes through Papa's eyes before he laughs it off and says, "Well, you'll not mind if I have another wee shottie myself." He proceeds to do so, humming a wee tune (*Oh, I remember that wee tune!*) and pretending everything is fine.

What is going on? This is ridiculous! I would NEVER treat Papa like this!

But I did.

This is not some new illusion created by Things-of-Water for his own mischievous amusement. This is not an echo from some strange, parallel Skerrils.

This is a Saturday afternoon, when Callum was eight. And this is exactly how it happened.

Callum now remembers every detail, knows what's coming, knows he cannot change it. He was bored and cross that day. He was supposed to be going into Oban with Steven and his family for a day trip, but his dad had stopped him because he'd made a bow and arrow, shot it in the garden (despite being told not to) and smashed a pane of the neighbour's greenhouse. He'd stormed out in a huff, eventually ending up at Papa's house, and the old man had wanted to take Callum's mind off it with a wee fishing trip.

Which was exactly like him. Callum had taken it so much for granted, this ally that he had, this kind old soul who never judged or punished him. He had appreciated it; he *knows* he had appreciated it. It's what he's missed so horribly over the last few months.

But he had also forgotten it, countless times, in the day-to-day stooshie of existence.

On this day, this perfect day, living a life that some of the city kids he now goes to school with would imagine came out of a picture book, all Callum could think about was how unfair it was that he wasn't away with Steven. He'd dutifully cast his rod a couple of times, caught nothing and got fed up. It was sunny but a bit cold out on the water, and he'd blamed Papa for his discomfort. He hadn't *wanted* to spend the day with Papa. It wasn't fair.

Why THIS day? Why not later, when I needed him? Why not…

But this is a thankless line of thought, as day after day of carelessness parades across his memory—taking routes that didn't pass Papa's house because he couldn't be bothered going in to talk. Not being interested in Papa's interests, sharing no love for fixing things, for watercolours, for classical music, for writing. Forgetting birthdays (*he's old, he won't* mind). He tries to conjure a memory that shows the relationship was equal, that he was as thoughtful and generous to Papa as Papa had been to him, but there is nothing, nothing but the realisation that the man who would drop everything to cater to Callum's well-being must have done so in the knowledge that his grandson was a selfish wee nyaff.

In his mind, Callum is screaming, sobbing, begging Papa for forgiveness, while his eight-year-old body says, "I'm cold. Can we go in now?"

"Just a moment, laddie," says Papa, suddenly alert, "I think I've got a bite!" His line is taut, the reel begins to spin, and Papa whoops in delight.

Please, thinks Callum, *I don't need to see the rest of this. I remember what happened!*

Papa is now standing, knees bent to keep his balance in the shoogly wee boat, and fighting with whatever is on the end of the line. Sometimes he winds the reel in, sometimes he lets it run, and throughout the process he has a beatific smile on his weathered, old face.

"Come on now, wee fishie," he's saying. "Come on, my wee beauty!"

White foam forms around the sloshing boat, and Papa almost overbalances, recovering with a delighted, breathless laugh.

"The net, Callum!" he cries, and Callum knows what he's supposed to do, but he fumbles, feigning ignorance like a thrawn wee sulk.

"It's okay, laddie, just pass it to me!" Papa's voice is high with excitement. Callum passes him the net and sits back down, tutting at the splashes that come over the side and wet him. Papa, with the grace of an acrobat, tucks the rod under one arm while leaning forward with the net. For one terrified second, Callum recalls, he was sure the old man would fall in, though his concern was more to do with how inconvenient that would be for him than for Papa's safety. After all, the old man used to joke about how he liked doing lengths in the Atlantic.

Papa recovers, scoops a ten-pound sea bass out of the sea, and lays it reverently in the keel of the boat where it fights and thrashes helplessly. There is sweat pouring down Papa's forehead, his cheeks are red and he is breathless.

"My grateful thanks," he says to the sea, then turns, smiling, to Callum. "That'll do for our tea tonight, Callum! What do you think? Shall we cook him over a bonfire on the shore?"

Please take me away from here now. Please. Please let me change this, let me say, "Yes." Let me sit with my wonderful grandfather on the beach, eating fresh cooked fish as the smoke from the bonfire rises to the stars. Let me be the grandson he deserves.

But the last battle with the sea bass had sent a skoosh of cold salt water across Callum's lap, and in a self-pitying fit of pique he leaned forward, scooped the gasping fish up in his hands and tossed it over the side to vanish beneath the sea sparkle.

Internally, Callum is torn to pieces. He wants to close his eyes, more, even, than he had wanted to hug Papa. He wants to close his eyes and forget the shame which he'd instantly felt on seeing Papa's reaction. He wants to close his eyes. But he can't, because he didn't. And there Papa stands, his mouth open in astonishment, finally slumping back onto his seat and looking from Callum to the widening circles in the surf in stunned disappointment.

I wish, dear reader, that I could tell you that was the worst of it, but it was not.

You see, as Callum now recalls, he had justified this heinous crime by claiming that he felt sorry for the fish. And Papa, despite being robbed of his tea, despite having been spoken to like a tiresome old inconvenience, despite having cared about the fish on a level young Callum could not have fathomed, believed him. He shared the story, told his friends and Callum's parents; grew proud of his grandson's good heart and strong convictions. It became part of the Folklore of Callum.

And Papa had never fished again.

"That is enough of that, now," says Elsa, reaching across impossible boundaries and taking Callum's hand. And here he is, back on the shore. The same shore, in a different time. A fisherman fishing, in a different time. And he collapses on the shingle in inconsolable grief. Jenny, without thinking, drops down next to him and throws her arms around him, and Callum returns the embrace, shaking in misery and wishing, *wishing* to be someone else.

The Other

B EYOND ALL THIS, undaunted by the part of it that is battling Things-of-Green, The Other is wearing a smile of grim satisfaction. In all its long, endless years, the snapping of connections, the breaking of the web, has been its sole delight. We need, perhaps, to know a little of its nature before we witness any more of its endeavours.

It is not, we now need to agree, an old man. Nor is it the same sort of being as Things-of-Green, Things-of-Blood and the others, whatever they may be. They are chaotic tangles of life, of mind, of consequence; The Other waits for all such things to end.

It is old, older than anything else we have met. It was here before here was here, *long* before. When all the blazing heat of Creation burst forth, The Other was already ancient and complete. While Things-of-Green has never known a world without it, to The Other, Things-of-Green is a trying child, intruding on its space and disrupting everything with his noise and nonsense. Perhaps we might think of it as Things-of-Cold, or Things-that-are-Not, for though it was born of empty stillness, it is present in all things. It's the silence between atoms that sound can't touch, the waiting, forgetful nothingness to which all things will return. It was, and is, and will be, not an enemy to be beaten but a fact we like to avoid. We carry it in us. Everyone who has longed for the good old days, who has seen their world changing and wished it would stop. Those iron-age villagers, the adults at least, pass the time by moaning about how much better things used to be. The stone-age tribespeople, in languages now long dead, worry that the young folks don't respect the old ways enough. We will all, in some quiet moment, wish that we could stop it all, and in that thought, The Other nods and waits.

This is the way of things. Without the thought that things will end, we would never know to take delight in the moment, to build a treasure trove of memories to guide us through dark times. In this, The Other is a friend to you and to me. But there are times when its patience starts to crack. When the noisy clamour of life and laughter leads it to abandon its nature and intervene, interfere, manifest as the very thing it isn't, a living presence. There are times when the knowledge that all will return to silence is not enough, and it wants to hasten the process. An old man mysteriously appearing in Skerrils, confusing the children and frightening the adults into silence, is not as strange as we might have thought. Similar things have happened in many places, in many times, often in moments of alarming change. Why here? Why now? Why Callum? Why Papa? Why Things-of-Green?

Excellent questions, you clever thing!

Well, it has been up and about for a while, busy in the world, delighted as people fold in upon themselves. It has watched with glee as we have done its work for it, as we wilfully sever our connections and pour scorn on those who look for common ground. Whenever someone tells you that you can't share a thought, it grows. Whenever someone tells you that you don't feel what others feel, it grows. Whenever the world tells you that people you admired were not as good as you thought, that times you enjoyed were not as good as you thought, that good luck and happy times are privileges to be ashamed of, it grows. Whenever you are tricked into believing that you are unique and that your job in life is to belligerently insist upon your uniqueness to the world. Whenever you see those who hold a version of you, one that you'd prefer to ignore, as hostile alien forces, rather than custodians of an important truth...

You get the idea.

As long as you believe that existence is good, there is nothing we can do that cannot come to good. As long as you believe that existence is bad, there is nothing we can do that cannot come to bad.

Things-of-Green, Things-of-Blood, Things-of-Stone and Things-of-Water all believe that existence is good, and so whatever chaos they may cause, whatever hearts they may break, whatever minds they may blow, however terrifying they may be, all will be well in their eyes. This is an alarming attitude to witness, but thrilling, exciting, intoxicating. Those lucky enough to share it firsthand, as Callum has, will never be bored in the world, though they may be heart-racingly terrified from time to time. They know in their bones that the fear, the joy, the consternation, the anticipation, the disappointment and the conflumixment are what make us One. Callum and his friends, and Papa, had seen this in a way few still can.

But The Other casts shadows in the firelight, waiting for the ash to grow cold and dead. It knows that every experience is one experience fewer on the way to silence. It haunts the thoughts of those that think; it is doubt and stasis and paralysis and inertia. It is the feeling that the things we do amount to nothing, that the purpose we find in life can be casually dismissed, that we can never truly bridge the gaps between us and that we are all, in the end, alone.

When it senses an advantage, it appears. It grows. It becomes hungry and animated and present in the world. When Callum suddenly lost his rudder in this world—Callum, whose adventures had been so momentous as to bring a whole town towards The One—The Other saw its chance. And now that Callum, under Things-of-Water's thoughtless spell, has started to see his most precious relationship as a source of shame and regret, The Other's satisfaction grows intense.

Why? Why can beings as powerful, magical and aware as Things-of-Green not banish this bleak force, cast it into the darkness it so clearly craves?

Well, you will have heard this before. You will have heard it before because it's true, I'm afraid.

It is because you cannot have One without The Other.

Comfort

"BEFORE YOU LOSE yourself in regrets, dear Callum, you should know there is a place," says Elsa, "where you failed. Every possible Skerrils is here, and you did not always succeed."

They are still on the shore, Callum and Jenny side by side in mutual reassurance and Elsa standing by the waterline, gazing out to sea. Callum has dried his eyes and taken a few deep breaths, brought back into himself by Jenny's easy kindness.

"What do you mean?" he asks. "What, when Papa was ill?"

Elsa nods.

Two summers ago, during Callum's first adventures with Things-of-Green, he had somehow managed to avert disaster, to keep The Mountain from leaving (whatever that meant) and, perhaps, keeping Papa from leaving too. He had sacrificed a world of personal wonder for a world where everyone knew, briefly, that magic was afoot and that every day was a blessing. And he had snatched a few more precious months with his beloved guide and mentor, watching him fade like an autumn leaf but grateful for every second.

"Would you like to see?"

"*What*?"

"Would you like to see? You are thinking that your love for your Papa was less than you'd imagined, that you did him no good. But I can show you a Skerrils where you did not try, and it is bleak and gaunt and grey."

"That sounds amazing," says Jenny. "I don't suppose you could take us to a Skerrils where there's a Ferris wheel and an ice rink, could you? Maybe some *shops* and things?" This draws a snort of bitter laughter from Callum and a raised eyebrow from Elsa.

"She's right," says Callum. "If we can move about freely, maybe we could give the old bleakness a body-swerve for a bit? I can imagine it well enough without seeing it."

Elsa smiles. "Yes. Jenny, you are wise. It is easy for me to forget that you are not used to this existence. I have been here a long time. Perhaps I have picked up some bad habits from Things-of-Green!"

Whichever reality they are currently sharing, it is beginning to get dark. The fisherman and his daughter have taken their catch happily back into the village, where smoke now rises through thatch as doors and shutters close against the night. The birdsong of dusk is carried from the wooded hillside on the still evening air, and everything feels so calm and solid and *real*, it's hard to believe that things could change with the click of the fingers.

"Elsa," says Callum, "how *have* you been here for so long? Are you stuck here or something?"

The old woman gazes up at the darkening sky, the slowly spreading blanket of stars, and she takes a deep breath.

"For that tale, *a ghràidh,* we need firelight," she says, and instantly a merry bonfire of driftwood springs up between them. It crackles and sparks, and Callum and Jenny, though surprised, are grateful for its warmth and light.

"She don't look to me like she's trapped, mate," says Jenny. "She looks to me like she runs the place!"

Elsa settles gracefully on the shingle, looking a little pleased with Jenny's observation. "Ah, not quite," she says, "but perhaps a little of both. You'd be surprised how addictive control can become. Callum, what did your Papa tell you about me?"

Callum rubs his chin thoughtfully. "Ehm, not that much, really. And you know, Mum's never even mentioned you." He is suddenly confused. "I don't know why I didn't think that was strange."

Jenny jabs him with her elbow. "Stick to the point," she says, and Callum gives himself a shoogle.

"Sorry, yeah. You know, there was one thing he told me. He said that when you all met Things-of-Green and the others, you know, when you were kids, he said that you got taken off to their weird land and were missing for a year, and that he was the only one who noticed!" Remembering the conversation briefly transports Callum to Papa's front room, to the smell of pipe smoke and the taste of sweet tea, and he finds he can't really continue with the story. Elsa gently takes up the tale.

"Well, yes," she says, "that is what he believed. But I wasn't *taken*, Callum. I *chose* to go. Your Papa could have done the same, if he'd realised it, but he was too attached to the land as he knew it.

"Tell me, when you first met our friends, how did it change you?"

This is a very big question and Callum struggles to find the words.

"It's weird," he says. "I think it was like it *hadn't* changed me. It just made me realise a lot of things which I'd never noticed before. It was like, I don't know, I could see under the surface of things, you know?" He breaks into a smile. "It was *amazing*, actually! A wee bit scary, but everything was so... So *beautiful*!"

Jenny is listening intently, her eyes bright in the firelight.

"You are so much like him." says Elsa. "Of all the ways we can respond, falling in love with the land is far from being the worst! And I know just what you mean. That glimpse beneath the surface is a wonderful thing. But I wanted more than to see it, Callum. I wanted to *be* in it. And so I went deeper."

"He was really worried about you, you know," says Callum. He feels oddly offended on Papa's behalf. "He couldn't tell anyone about it either. He worried about you for a whole year, with no-one to talk to! No-one in the town remembered you except him. Maybe his pals as well, but I think they were losing their marbles by that point."

There is a pause, Callum's accusation hanging in the air with the smoke from the fire, until at last, Elsa says, "Look."

She points at the fire, and there, slowly forming in the flames, comes a hazy view of Callum's Skerrils. The images dance and skirl together: Callum's mum, talking on the phone, swirling into the busy café; Steven leaning on the counter talking to Helen the waitress, whose bored indifference sparks and flickers. Then it is Jenny's mum, a book lying open on her lap as she gazes into space; the library, Mrs. Duguid locking up for the day; the old folks' home; Roy McKenzie hurrying across a street; a parade of random villagers going about their business. And then Vicky, whose

141

sudden appearance draws a gasp from Callum. Vicky is staring straight through the flames at him, looking lost and determined and mouthing words he cannot hear. Can she see him? It appears for all the world as if she is trying to. Callum is so startled by the image that he almost misses Elsa's next words.

"I never left him, really," she says. "I could see what he was going through. It is the only reason I returned." She doesn't sound sad, exactly, but there's something in her tone that drags Callum's gaze from the flickering images of home. Vicky's haunted, troubled face disappears in the glowing orange light.

Elsa shakes her head and smiles. "I am glad I went back, of course, for had I not done so, *you* would not be here, Callum. Your Papa and I were married, time passed, we had a child, and we knew that we could not raise her properly if we had one foot in this place. Babies are hard work, you know!

"We struck a deal. I would put aside my knowledge of the Mountain and devote myself to your mother. Your Papa could continue to be one with the landscape, to have the best of both worlds. Apart from anything else, it made him the best ghillie in the country, and that put food on the table! Women," she continues, giving Jenny a meaningful look, "have been striking such deals since the dawn of time, though they seldom get to negotiate with as clear a view as I had."

"Okay," says Jenny, "so what was your side of the bargain? I mean, apart from getting to play Mum for a while?"

Elsa ignores the jibe. "We agreed that when we were done—by which I mean, when Anna, Callum's mother, was old enough not to need us both any longer—I would be free to return here should I wish to. And when the time came..." She pauses, scrutinising Callum, perhaps curious about how he will take this. "When the time came, well, I wished to.

"Your mother has no memory of me, Callum, save for the fact that she knows she was loved."

The night is pierced by the lonely cry of an oystercatcher, lifting off the shoreline some distance to the west.

Callum jabs the fire with a stick, agitated, and a shower of sparks fly heavenwards.

"How do you *know* she knows that?" he demands. "How do you know she hasn't felt abandoned? Rejected?"

"I know," says Elsa softly, "because of how she loves *you*. We pass along the love we receive—the hatred too, I fear. And, Callum."

He looks up, meets her gaze.

"Your lie about the fish."

He gulps. He didn't know Elsa had witnessed that, and he'd been so caught up in her story that he'd briefly

143

forgotten it himself. He would have preferred to keep it that way.

"You turned it into a truth," she says.

He looks at her blankly.

"It doesn't matter why you threw the fish back, really. What matters is that you knew why your Papa *thought* you threw it back. And you spent the next four years trying to live up to that idea. Lesser children would have forgotten about it or would have thought well of their own cleverness at pulling off a successful deception. But you couldn't bear to disappoint your Papa.

"What started as pretence, the hiding of a lie, became a real, bone-deep love of Nature, of the world around you. You became a boy who really *couldn't* bear to see a fish drawing its last breath, to see an animal in distress. Your Papa could not have been more proud of you. And Things-of-Green would never have noticed you if it had happened any other way.

"Do not be deceived by a single memory, dear heart. Memories must be set in place, like jewels upon a crown. They have no meaning without the stories they are part of, and the stories are always far bigger than you imagine.

"Now. Night draws in. Where do we wish to go next?"

PingMe

SUNLIGHT GLANCES OFF the Mountain, leaving Callum and Jenny half-blind as well as totally disorientated. The glare is not bouncing off scree, nor glinting from the dancing waters of the burns that tumble off the crags. It is not joining birdsong and lapping waves in the clear Skerrils air.

No.

It is reflecting off rows, blocks, *acres* of metallic buildings which now sprout like barnacles across its surface, and the air is filled with city noise, rumbling, booming, bizarre. There is a haze in the air, the haze of industry, so they cannot even see the top of the Mountain. They can see, however, that there is a cable and, suspended from it, pods like spaceships ascending sedately to who-knows-what at the summit. Drones zip and fly around on unknown errands, one pausing above them unnervingly, as if checking them out, before disappearing.

Iron-age Skerrils has dissolved in the glare. They have shifted scene yet again, and it would be fair to say it is beginning to fray Jenny's nerves. They're still on the shore, but the shore is a gleaming concrete marina, and the view out to sea is blocked by countless luxurious boats of the sort that might look more at home in Monaco or Miami. The shore road is now a glinting dual carriageway, and rather than ending in the familiar gritty cul-de-sac of Callum's Skerrils, it crosses the shining arc of a bridge that spans the bay and alights on MacArthur's Island. Just visible through the haze, Callum sees that the island, too, is covered in buildings, all glass and chrome and dazzle.

"Where... What... *When...*?" he stammers. This is alien. He might as well have fetched up on the surface of Mars. Plasma-screen billboards adorn the glistening buildings which stand where his hometown should be, showing smiling models promoting the virtues of everything from shampoo to electric cars to life insurance. Tinny jingles echo through the streets, playing, it seems, to no-one, for the one thing Callum cannot see in this unsettling technological wonderland is *people*. He assumes they must be in the buildings and in the tinted-windowed vehicles that hum past at high speed on the wide, winding road, but so far there is no sign of another actual person out of doors.

Disconcertingly, Elsa looks just as at home here as she has everywhere else.

"When is this?" Callum demands. "Is this, like, the twenty-third century or something?"

"It is *now*, Callum," Elsa replies. "Everywhere we have been is now. But I suppose," she adds, raising a hand to acknowledge Callum's frustration, "from your perspective, this is, perhaps, twenty years in your future."

"Twenty *years*?" cries Callum. "What the hell happened? Where did Skerrils go?" He looks around frantically, searching in vain for some familiar landmark, for some sign of the pure green pulse he knows from his beloved landscape.

"Well," says Elsa, "Jenny *did* want to see some shops, did she not?"

This draws an incredulous laugh from both Callum and Jenny, and in a spirit of hopeless resignation, they agree to do a little exploring. The three of them turn from the busy sea and walk into town. There is no easy route, as the roads do not have proper pavements, and they need to hug the concrete sidings to avoid being run over by the speeding vehicles. Callum mutters under his breath the whole time—"This is nuts! This is insane! This is mental!"—and it would be getting on Jenny's nerves if she didn't completely agree.

At last, they come to a point where the road vanishes into a labyrinthine indoor space, probably a car park, and a wide-open plaza gives them their first view of actual people. Moving walkways circle the space, and there are folk being whisked about on them, into and out of shops and cafés, up to high storeys through glass-fronted buildings. It's a giddying sight, and sort of exciting, but the strange thing is that the people themselves look, for the most part, totally unimpressed.

"They're not even talking to each other," says Jenny, giving voice to the thought that had been puzzling Callum.

It's true. The figures, mostly youthful, smartly dressed people with an air of good health about them, are being shunted passively about with glazed eyes as if there couldn't possibly be anything of interest in their immediate surroundings.

"I mean," Jenny goes on, "just seeing this many people must be mind-blowing for you, Callum, but I know cities, and this would be weird even in London!"

It's difficult to focus with the cacophony of advertising, the constant zipping of drones in and out of his peripheral vision, but Callum is desperate to make sense of the scene. He scans the whole space and notices a statue in the middle that looks as if it might have a plaque at its base.

"Let's go over there," he says, setting off at a trot with Jenny and Elsa following behind.

The statue is of two men, standing back-to-back in heroic pose. It's not an unusual bit of civic art, except that instead of wearing the uniform of some bygone age and holding swords or rifles aloft, the two men are wearing hard hats, hi-vis vests, jeans and steelies. One is holding a pickaxe, the other a shovel.

"It can't be," says Jenny, arriving at Callum's side.

"Look at this!" he says, and they look at the faded plaque at the statue's base. It is made of tarnished metal, but the words are still clear enough. They read them together.

"*In memory of Wullie and Brian. They gave their lives that we might PING!*"

Just as they turn to gaze at each other in speechless astonishment, a sleek, black vehicle comes whirring alongside them and screeches to a halt. Elsa, who has joined them, steps defensively between the children and the vehicle.

"Stay behind me," she says, and though her voice is as gentle and lilting as ever, Callum senses she is uneasy. This is not a comforting thought.

"Can they see us?" hisses Jenny. "Whoever's in that thing. Can they see us?"

"No idea," says Callum. "Doesn't look like anyone can see *anyone* here. Look at them all!" The well-dressed shoppers continue to be ferried around the walkways, but their eyes are as glazed as the statues'. Occasionally, someone will touch their ear and smile, but it doesn't seem to relate to anything going on around them.

At last, a door hisses open on the side of the vehicle, revealing a plush leather interior with four large figures inside. There doesn't seem to be a driver, so Callum assumes the vehicle drives itself. There is, however, plenty of room for three more, so when one of the figures rasps, "Get in!" he can see no reason not to do so. He looks at Jenny, who shrugs, and Elsa, who purses her lips but nods, and the three of them clamber in.

Whoever these four are, they are clearly obscenely well-off. They sit, bloated and comfortable, in individual leather seats, each with some piece of finery of his own. One has a rich fur collar on his pinstripe suit, which shouldn't really work but seems to. Another is clutching a cane of dark, expensive wood—mahogany, Callum supposes—and has a lurid pink carnation peeking from his buttonhole. The third is resplendent in a flowing blue silk gown and holds a crystal glass of some clear, sparkling liquid in his pudgy hand. The fourth, a rather grim forbidding fellow, sports a tie pin with a diamond the size of a pigeon's egg upon it. The door slides silently shut behind them as Callum, Jenny and Elsa settle awkwardly into their own leather seats and the four figures eye them expectantly.

"Um," says Callum, since no-one else is talking. "Who are you?"

The four figures erupt in wheezy laughter.

"Who are we?" chuckles Fur Collar to the others. "Who are we, indeed? How soon they forget, eh?"

Pink Carnation shakes his head, a condescending smile spreading across a face as pink as the flower. He clicks his fingers and the vehicle begins to move, to Callum's slight alarm.

"Oh, Callum Maxwell," says the man as the view outside shows they are speeding quietly back towards the bridge to MacArthur's Island. "Are we really so strange to you?" He pulls a huge cigar from an inside pocket and lights it, filling the car with acrid smoke. Callum is banjaxed. *Maybe*, he thinks, *these are folk I know in my time?* But they don't resemble any of his friends in the tiniest way. Although...

No.

No, it absolutely *can't* be.

Elsa breaks the silence.

"You have changed, Things-of-Green," she says sadly. Jenny gasps as they race over the glittering waves, and Callum closes his eyes in horror and confusion.

Steven

"CHANGED," SIGHS THINGS-OF-GREEN.

Callum opens his eyes reluctantly and looks at the enormous man before him. All four of them, in fact—the living, magical embodiments of the world he knows and loves, buttoned into suits, decadent, comfortable. It's just so incongruous, like a monkey on a bicycle. They shouldn't be in here, in this sterile, high-tech vehicle. They belong outside, wild and majestic. It can't be them.

And yet, as he looks between them, he thinks he can detect some remnant of that fizzing brilliance. Although they have the bodies of overfed businessmen, their eyes retain a certain sparkle. And, after all, Callum has seen them as plants, as boulders, as waterfalls, as seabirds—why *shouldn't* they take this form too?

Things-of-Green seems to have read his mind. He smiles.

"Change is what we *do*, Lady Elsa," he says, though he's holding Callum's gaze. "Are you happier with *these* shapes?" At once, with no visible movement, all four are the shimmering pliskies that Callum first met, radiating mischief and ancient, unknowable secrets. "Or *these* ones?" Now, disconcertingly, they are the stern giants that Callum once witnessed stalking away from Skerrils as a tide of emptiness swept over it in the wake of Papa's heart attack. They're very hard to look at, as they seem to be several times larger than the car they are in while still fitting comfortably in their leather seats.

"Stop!" cries Jenny. "Seriously, whatever you are, *who*ever you are, please stop it! I'm losing my mind here!"

Callum reaches out, and she takes his hand distractedly. Her knee is bouncing in agitation, and Callum realises that all of this is far weirder for her than it is for him, and it's pretty blinking weird for him.

"For now," rumbles Things-of-Stone, "we are content in these forms." And Callum, Jenny and Elsa are once again confronted with the vision of four wealthy, well-dressed human men.

The car has sped across the bridge's glittering span, and they are now winding along a narrow road that leads through a neighbourhood of glass-panelled houses, up to the peak of the island's small hill. The car slows itself as they approach a black cast iron gate, set in a whitewashed wall so high they can't make out what is beyond it. The gate is wrought in a nautical theme, with seashell patterns bordering the outline of an old-fashioned sailing ship. They have no real time to admire this, however, before the gate hums silently open and the car proceeds up a wide, winding driveway. Giant flowering shrubs line the route, an endless, immaculate lawn stretching off behind them. They are approaching the most opulent house Callum has ever laid eyes on.

It is built into the living rock of the hill. It dazzles in the sunlight, endless windows in every direction and balconies with shining silvery bannisters. There are fountains in the garden, a helicopter hunched like a vulture on the flat roof, a garage several times the size of Callum's own house. The folds and contours of the island's summit flow seamlessly into the house's architecture, as if the hill was made to be lived in. An outdoor pool glistens off to one side, which is impressive, though Callum suspects there are probably only about four days a year when it's warm enough to swim in it. Whoever lives here must not be someone who cares too much about practicality.

The car hums to a stop, the door slides open, and the four strange figures are now standing outside awaiting them.

"And what are we doing here?" Elsa asks, stepping gracefully onto the paving slabs. Jenny and Callum jump out behind her, instantly struck by the salty sea air and the view back over the water to Skerrils and the Mountain. With a little distance, Callum has to admit that it is still his hometown: the rise of the land, the curve of the shore, hold fast despite the pace of change.

"We are here to show we have *won*," says Things-of-Blood. "We are strangers to your kind no more, and you need never again fear disconnection!"

The house is even more impressive close up. The front doors, glass like everything else, are monogrammed with ornate letters—an 'S' on the left and a 'C' on the right. Before Callum has time to wonder what this means, the doors slide open, and Things-of-Water leads the way indoors. A vast, sunlit, stone-floored room greets them, with winding glass staircases leading up into various open-plan levels. There are huge soft couches big enough to park your car on, a tropical fish tank that Callum could swim in, a well-stocked bar and a full-sized snooker table. The views out across the sea are stunning. Whoever lives here is doing very, very well.

A voice can be heard from an upstairs room, and they all move as one, drawn towards the first sign of life. They climb a gleaming staircase and follow the sound along a landing, their steps muffled by a thick, soft carpet. They pass room after room until they come to an open door and peer into a huge, luxurious office. A highly polished wooden conference table occupies the middle of the floor, and banks of screens fill every wall. Some of these show graphs and charts, some are silently running news channels from around the world, and some, it has to be said, are showing cartoons. One wide window on the back wall gives a vista down the hill to the far side of the island; it's quite a giddying drop and a view that Callum feels should trump the telly every time.

There is a man in the room, sitting with his feet up on the table. He's talking loudly, though Callum can't see a device. The pauses suggest he is having a conversation, so unless he's talking to the voices in his head, there must be a connection to someone somewhere.

"Aye, aye," he's saying, "next Monday will be fine. Any later, though, and the contract's terminated. Thanks, darlin'! Aye, you too! Ciao!" He grabs a fistful of nuts from a bowl on the table and pops them into his mouth, munching messily and happily. "Eejits," he mutters, nut crumbs flying from his lips.

Things-of-Green, mahogany cane in hand, marches over to the seated man, followed by his fellows. Things-of-Blood lays a hand on the man's shoulder. The man reacts but doesn't look at any of them. He closes his eyes and gives a deep, contended sigh.

It's Steven.

Twenty years older, richer than he could ever have wished, but gallus and glaikit as Callum remembers him. And then Callum realises that the fine chair upon which Steven is reclining is the wooden throne he once sat upon at the bottom of the sea—one made of the remnants of countless makeshift boats which had failed to carry him, as an enthusiastic laddie, across to MacArthur's Island.

"Well," says Callum, shaking his head, "I suppose you made it across in the end."

"This one was always willing," says Things-of-Water. "Do you wish to speak with him?"

Callum is startled. "What? He won't know me, will he?"

Things-of-Water tilts his head. "He will speak to you," he says, "but he will not know you."

Before Callum can decide, four of the screens on the wall start flashing, and Steven curses under his breath. He hits some hidden console on the table before him, and the screens coalesce into a single image. A face.

Craig.

"Ma man!" says Steven, "How's Hong Kong?"

Craig scowls out of the screen, thrawn as ever. "Too hot," he snaps. Steven laughs.

"Well," he says. "Ah did offer tae go, didn't ah? But your second-in-command wisnae good enough for the Chinese! So, have ye sold them on PingMe yet, wi yer winning charm?"

Craig brightens slightly. "Oh, yes," he says, and Callum notices that Craig's accent has changed. He sounds sort of half-American for some reason. "They've signed up. They didn't have much choice with every other network folding!"

Steven stretches and puts his hands behind his head, a look of total satisfaction on his face.

"That's it then," he says. "Total market dominance! Jeezo, mah old pal, wha'd hae thunk it, eh? You comin' back tae Skerrils, then?"

Craig snorts. "That dump? I don't think so. I just wanted to make sure the theme park development was going well."

"Pingland?" says Steven. "Oh, aye. Proper cheesefest it'll be an aw—*Feel the couthy warmth o' the toon that started it aw*—ye ken the kinna hing. We even got permission tae shift the Holy Cairn fae the foot o' McKenzie's field tae the tap o' the Mountain. We've made displays sayin' it wis there aw alang. The Yanks'll lap it up, it'll hae authenticity comin' oot its oxters. But listen," he adds, looking serious for the first time, "ye should come. It'd be good tae see ye. Ah dae miss ye, ye ken."

Craig's expression softens for a moment, and he even sounds briefly Scottish again. "Aye, ah miss you an aw," he says, then corrects himself. "I miss you too. We'd some good times, eh?"

"That we did! Stuff the world widnae believe if we telt them!"

"Stuff *I* don't really believe if I'm honest. I don't suppose..."

"What?"

"Oh, nothing." Craig looks embarrassed. Steven smiles—a sad smile, Callum thinks.

"Ye're wonderin' if there's ony news, eh. Aboot Vicky."

Callum is suddenly alert. The mention of Vicky has sent an unexpected pang through him, and Craig looks similarly affected.

"And is there?"

Steven shakes his head.

"'Fraid not, bud," he says. "Whitiver it wis she went aff tae find, she husnae felt the need tae ask for ma help."

This is too much for Callum, who jumps forward and slams a hand on the table's polished surface. Steven starts in astonishment.

"Who the..." he begins, but Callum interrupts him.

"What happened to Vicky?" he demands. Steven has leapt to his feet.

"How in the hell did you get in here?" he asks.

On screen, Craig looks alarmed. "What's happening? Where's your security?"

And then, still unnoticed by Steven or Craig, Things-of-Blood steps forward and speaks into Steven's ear.

"This is a friend," he says.

Steven pauses, and a glazed look comes over him. "You are a friend," he says to Callum.

"You can answer his questions," says Things-of-Blood.

"I'll answer your questions," says Steven.

Craig vanishes from the screen, perhaps too busy to worry about a little madness in his distant hometown. Callum is elated and turns to grin at his companions. Elsa is smiling in encouragement, but Jenny is now sitting on the carpet and shaking her head, muttering, "Okay. Any second now, I'm gonna wake up." This is troubling, but Callum has the sense of a moment about to pass and he needs to press ahead. And so, he turns back to speak to his dear old friend.

Unsafe

I T IS A sad truth about the world that fourteen-year-old boys are seldom invited into the offices of high-flying executives to demand answers to their crazy questions, and yet somehow Callum feels as if this is a perfectly normal situation. It is not, after all, the first time he has had to press Steven to pay attention to a serious issue. And although this version of Steven does not, apparently, know who Callum is, he relaxes into the moment with surprising ease, settling back on his ridiculous wooden throne and meeting Callum's gaze obediently.

"Vicky," says Callum again. "What happened to her?"

"Ah dinnae ken," says Steven. "She wis a pal o' mine when I wis wee, but she vanished nearly twenty years ago."

"What do you mean, 'vanished'?" It occurs to Callum that Vicky might have done an Elsa—jumped over into the world of Things-of-Green—but if that were so, Steven shouldn't have any memory of her.

"She went aff on a mission," says Steven. "She wis lookin' for something, or someone, but she couldnae tell us whit it wis."

"And what, you just let her *go*?" Callum is angry. The thought of Vicky coming to harm has set off alarms in every part of him, a fear as great as anything he's faced in the last few days.

"Look, son, Ah cannae see whit it's got tae dae wi you, but it wisnae exactly oot o' character, ye ken? She wisnae someone wha'd convene a board meeting afore she made her decisions." He peers at Callum more closely. "How dae you even ken aboot her, anyway? Ye're whit, thirteen? Fourteen? She disappeared afore you were even born!"

The fight is draining from Callum with every word. He feels hopeless.

"You really don't know me, do you?" he asks.

Steven narrows his eyes. "Naw. Unless... You're no' a pal o' Callum's, are ye?"

"What?!" yells Callum. "I *am* Callum! Steven, look at me! It's me, Callum!"

The man sitting across from him recoils a little, looking a bit offended. "You're no' my son, son," he says, "an if ye carry on wi that nonsense, Ah'll hae ye chucked oot!"

At this point, Jenny gets up and leaves the room, muttering, "He called his son Callum. This just gets better and better."

Things-of-Green appears at Callum's side, his form somewhere between the aging businessman and the wild creature of wood and fern that Callum knows of old.

"You are not present here, Callum Maxwell," he says, his voice a sad sigh like the wind through a field of ripe barley. "He would know you if you were. Connection is total."

"We are losing each other." Elsa's tone is decisive. "We should stay together." She waves her hand, and at once they are standing outside again, Jenny by their side and Things-of-Green and the others looking rather put out. Steven's voice drifts out of the house, straight back on another call, their conversation forgotten.

"This is a Skerrils I do not know," Elsa says to Things-of-Green. "You will inform us what is going on."

Callum is astonished at her command of the situation. Jenny seems beyond caring, agitated and pale.

Things-of-Green, looking oddly diminished, responds. "We told you. We have won. We have forged a connection, not just in Skerrils, but across the whole world!"

"You mean *PingMe*?" cries Callum. "You're to blame for those stupid bloody noises everyone was so excited by?"

Things-of-Water steps forward, his blue silk gown flowing in the breeze. "We did not create it," he says, "but we saw it unfolding. It would have unfolded anyway, with us or without us."

"We took steps," adds Things-of-Blood, "to ensure it unfolded *with* us."

Callum is baffled.

"He means," says Jenny in a small, tight voice," that they kidnapped those poor men. Wullie and Brian. They've tangled their world with ours." She sounds disgusted. Callum knows where she's coming from.

"But *why?*" he demands. "This is nothing like you! These buildings, these cars, the screens, the tech—it's all so *artificial*!"

Things-of-Stone rumbles into speech.

"Artificial?" he growls. "What do you take us for, Callum Maxwell? The wires that drive your machines are forged from our essence! The satellites that share your thoughts around this world, they are launched with power we stored millennia ago! We are in the wind and the tides, the splitting cells and crumbling Mountain—how could we not be in this? We *are* connection! You think you ridiculous apes could create a world that does *not* have us in it?"

"We thought," adds Things-of-Green a little peevishly, "you would be pleased!"

Callum is nonplussed. He looks at Jenny, but she is too distressed to respond. Elsa is grim.

"So where am I?" asks Callum quietly. "Steven doesn't know me. I'm not in this Skerrils. I don't get back home, do I?"

"This is but one of many futures, dear heart," Elsa answers. Callum doesn't know how to take this.

"I suppose," he says at last, "that at least The Other hasn't won? I mean, if everyone's connected? I suppose that's a *good* thing, really? I suppose...I suppose we might be safe here?"

The salt air swirls around them, a sudden chill in its wake, as Jenny gives a snort of derision.

"You saw those people back there in the town. Riding about like zombies. Did they look connected to you?"

The chill intensifies. Jenny's words have struck a chord, not only with Callum but with Elsa, Things-of-Green and the others. They all exchange glances as the light changes around them. The air begins to tingle, then fizz, then snap with a static crackle, and Callum feels his gaze drawn inexorably over the water to the Mountain.

The cold wind has cleared the haze, and there it stands, ancient and huge. Behind it, it seems, a blackening storm cloud is rising.

And rising.

Blotting out the sun.

And it is not a storm cloud.

Rising, relentless, over a Skerrils entangled with every corner of the world, is the terrifying gargantuan figure of The Other. Light falls out of the sky around him, and it stands, a monstrous, ancient entity, devouring hope, devouring warmth, casting shadows of despair between Callum and his friends, between all the living beings on the crowded, vandalised mountainside. It raises its head and opens a mouth that looks like a hole in the sky, a black, swallowing void, and it roars with laughter. It spreads its hands like the host of a demonic feast, proud of the vista its hungry shadow falls over, a shadow that races across the bay and swamps the island in hopeless mirk.

Then it leans over, over the Mountain, dwarfing it completely in its bleak delight. Its eyes, its terrible, lifeless eyes, are gazing straight at Callum in cold, ravenous triumph.

Things-of-Green, Things-of-Blood, Things-of-Water and Things-of-Stone are chaotic, frantic, flickering around as insubstantial as light glancing off the ocean's troubled surface. Jenny has her eyes tight shut, her hands over her ears and her mouth open in a long and piercing scream. Callum is paralysed.

Elsa moves swiftly, grabs both of the children by their collars and says, "Stop."

And everything obeys.

Parting

I T'S AN OORIE sight. The Other's massive form hanging like the ash from a volcano, completely still, in the sky. Startled birds, motionless in the air, waves half-crashed on the shore below. When Callum jumps back in astonishment, his shadow remains where it was, glued to the ground, and Things-of-Green and the others are as rigid as figures in a mural, faces frozen in slapstick panic. Jenny, finally all screamed out, unclenches her eyes and lowers her hands from her ears. Judging from her reaction, the view that meets her isn't offering much comfort. In fact, unpleasant though it is to record, she runs to one of the flowering shrubs and boaks vigorously in its shade.

Elsa waits.

Callum gabbles. There are two conflicting thoughts in his mind. First, that nowhere is safe, and that even in a time of super-connection, The Other seems stronger than ever. Second, Elsa is so mind-bendingly powerful that in fact, everywhere is safe as long as he's with her. There's no way to fit both these thoughts into a single question, though, and the best he can manage is, "*How?*"

Jenny staggers back to his side looking green and miserable. "It's her, innit?" she says, her voice dry and cracking. "All of this. Haven't you noticed? It's all her."

Still, Elsa waits.

Callum shakes his head. "That doesn't make any sense," he says, but the control Elsa has over everything is staring him in the face.

"Look, mate," says Jenny, "you said you'd met *them* before, right?" She points at the ridiculous, static figures of Things-of-Green, Things-of-Blood, Things-of-Stone and Things-of-Water. Callum nods.

"Right," she continues, "well, I'm betting you were never able to make them do *that,* were you?" She goes over to the four figures, waves her hand in Things-of-Stone's face. There is no response. Things-of-Blood's right hand is outstretched, frozen in position as he flapped around in fright. Jenny reaches up to it, grasps it—no response. She pulls on it, and this unknowable entity which she's seen transform from hairy stone-age villager to weasel to futuristic corporate fat-cat, tips forward and lands flat on his face, still as rigid as a clothes-shop mannequin.

Callum finds this terribly upsetting. "Stop that!" he cries. "You're making them look ridiculous!" He can't bear to see them exposed as powerless or unimportant. These beings have been maddening, yes, but they've shaped his understanding of a world that is now slipping from his grasp. Things-of-Blood lying vulnerable on the ground is as painful a sight as Papa, baffled, watching his prize catch disappear beneath the waves.

"*I'm* not making them look ridiculous, Callum, that's the point! It's *her*!" Jenny turns on Elsa. "Look, *he's* never gonna ask you, so I'm just gonna come right out and say it. What, exactly, are you playing at?"

At last, Elsa responds. She smiles.

"Right now, I suppose, I am playing for time. Or *with* time. It amounts to the same thing." She looks at Callum. "I am not attempting to upset you, *a ghràidh*, and I share your concern for our friends there." She glides over to the prone figure of Things-of-Blood and lifts him effortlessly back to his feet.

"That doesn't really help," mutters Callum. "He still looks ridiculous."

"Yes," Elsa agrees, "but so does *that*." She waves a hand back towards the mainland, and all three look across the water. Sure enough, if anything, The Other looks even sillier than Things-of-Blood, all its ravening, noisy monstrosity caught like a mosquito in amber. Callum gives a shudder—it is still an ugsome brute by any measure—but he doesn't feel as if it's about to make a meal of him as he had only moments before.

"And *why*, exactly, are you 'playing for time'?" Jenny is as angry as she is curious.

"Because my grandson *needs* time, dear heart."

Jenny snorts. "Okay, *fine*. Callum needs time. But *how* can you give that to him? Why have *you* got *this* much power?"

By this point, Callum is getting tired of his helpless confusion and feels he should perhaps join in.

"Good question," he says. "Jenny's right. We're in the middle of this lunatic wonderland, crashing through time zones, running from *that* thing and caught up in *those* guys' nonsense again, but *you* just drift happily through it all! You click your fingers and everything changes! In fact, it was *you* who brought me in here in the first place! How? How do you do all this stuff?"

"I have no power that you do not also have, Callum." To add to his already considerable confusion, Callum detects a note of disappointment in Elsa's voice. "I can do this," she says, waving vaguely at the frozen figures. "I can move freely. I can guide you along, simply because I *choose* to do so. I *chose* to come here in the first place, remember? I am no-one's puppet, dear heart, to be toyed with and manipulated. This world is a tangle of infinite paths. Without the strength to choose your own, you will quickly get lost."

"So you can do *anything*?" Callum gazes at her and for the first time sees her as something rather frightening.

"No. No, not at all. That would not require a choice, now, would it? When faced with two paths, Callum, you can either choose one, the other, or none at all, but whatever way you choose to go, you also choose which way you *cannot* go. No-one is in complete control, here or anywhere else. *No-one* is free to do *anything*. But I..." She pauses, shrugs, and smiles. "I am at least willing to do *something*."

Callum's mouth opens and closes stupidly as he tries to form an answer. He can't help but feel that he is being criticised somehow, and the fact that he doesn't know how to answer feels as if he might be proving Elsa's point. Jenny is not so affected.

"How do you know your choice is right?" she asks quietly.

"I do not. I cannot. But I will see, and learn. It is easier here than it is outside, where you are buffeted by others' plans and dreams. I think...I think I found that too tiring. I think that is why I came here."

"So, what?" cries Callum. "What am I supposed to do? *I* don't know what I want to choose! And if I did, it wouldn't matter! Things keep happening that I don't want to happen! I didn't want Papa to die! I didn't want Vicky to leave Skerrils! I didn't want that hideous old man to kidnap Jenny! I don't want to get on the bus to Oban every day! I don't *want* to! I don't *have* a choice!"

"I do," says Jenny, and this puts Callum's gas at a peep. He stares at her. "I'm going home," she says. She turns to Elsa. "I think I understand, but this is your world, not mine. I choose to go home. I miss me mum."

Elsa gives a nod of approval.

Callum slumps to the ground, defeated, dejected. "It can't be that easy!" he says. "I only came here to get you!"

"Well," says Jenny, settling next to him, "you got me. You got me, but we're still here. I do appreciate it, Callum, I *really* do. God knows what would've happened if you'd not followed. But we're here, now, and we can choose to go home. Are you coming?"

Callum makes a noise, but his throat is choked up and it makes no sense.

"Come on, mate!" Jenny gives him a nudge. "There's no place like home! Click them ruby slippers together! Mission accomplished! There's no place like home!"

Callum gives a deep, shuddering sigh, and a big snottery sniff. "It... It's not..."

Jenny rubs his back encouragingly. "Not what, mate?"

Callum blinks at her, and a wee wet tear spills down his cheek. "It's not home anymore," he says.

Jenny gives him a sad smile. "Okay," she says, "I get it, I think. Maybe I'll see you around if you change your mind."

And she kisses his cheek, and is gone.

Map

A CRACKING.
A groaning, sickening rent.

Things are beginning to move again.

"Callum, you must make a decision," says Elsa urgently. "Time will not be held up for long."

Things-of-Green's fingers begin to flutter. Things-of-Blood turns his head, inch by aching inch. A slow, low boom, just on the edge of hearing, signals the waves unfolding painfully on the shore below. And in the sky above, the gargantuan hungry figure resumes its deadly advance, relentless and glacial.

"I don't know what to do!" shouts Callum. "There's nowhere to go that's safe! We're taking this thing with us wherever we go!"

"Yes, of course," says Elsa, "but we can keep it in its place if we decide to! *Where*, Callum? Will you return to your Skerrils with Jenny?"

The waves are louder now, crashing and booming, and the disturbance in the atmosphere rolls deafeningly around them as a peal of thunder.

"I *can't*!" Callum has to shout to be heard. Things-of-Green and the others are all moving freely again, shifting between forms at giddying, terrified speed. "I'm not strong enough to keep it in its place! I want a place without it!"

Things-of-Stone appears at his side, a figure made of shifting, swirling sand. He is trying to say something, but The Other drowns it out with its air-splitting roar. Things-of-Stone's movements become more and more agitated, and now Things-of-Water joins him, and Things-of-Blood, and Things-of-Green. Through their shape-shifting clanjamfry, Callum detects a desperation: they are using every ounce of their strength to tell him something, but before his despairing eyes, they become less and less substantial. They are diminishing, thinning out, fading into transparency, and with them goes Callum's sense of connection with the ground he stands on.

"What are they saying?" he yells to Elsa. She is bracing herself against a rising wind, arm over her eyes to shield against the flying dust, her jaw set in determination.

"It doesn't matter!" she shouts. "It is not their decision to make!" This has the most startling effect on the four swirling, vanishing beings. With the last of their remaining essence, they flow and swirl into a single form, animal, plant, rock and rain but somehow unmistakably human. This thing extends a furry, grassy arm and presses something into Callum's open palm.

"A place without him!" it says, then it peels itself apart and scatters on the wind. With it goes the last of Callum's love for the land, the last imagined tie to the boy he was.

Elsa has fought her way to Callum, and together they look at the thing he has been passed. It is a folded sheet of paper, or parchment, dazzlingly white, and he has to hold it tight to prevent it whipping out of his hand on the cold, cruel wind. He is beyond hope now, but a little part of him thinks maybe this paper will give a hint, a clue, as to what he should do. *A place without him*? Could it be a map, a route to sanctuary?

With Elsa's help, he unfolds it, his heart in his throat, and they survey it in the last of the lowering light.

It is completely blank. Not a mark or a blemish on its cool, white surface.

Elsa squeezes Callum's shoulder, an unusual sign of affection.

"You see?" she cries over the roaring tumult. "It is nothing. They cannot help. It was not their decision—"

"No," interrupts Callum. "I understand. It is a place *without him*. And without the dark, there's nothing. No colour, no form. That's what they mean. If I want to escape him, I have to give it all up.

"I want to go there. I've chosen.

"Take me there."

Elsa meets his gaze, and Callum sees that she suddenly looks ancient and tired, but she nods, takes his hand and then

A voice says, "Where are we?"

A voice answers, "A place without Him."

Silence.

The first voice says, "But I am still Callum."

The second voice says, "And I am still Elsa."

Silence.

"Why am I still Callum?"

"Because I am still with you to know that you are Callum."

Silence.

"Then please.

"Please,

just leave me alone

Alone

Edgeless, formless I

Colourless, empty I

Free, I free

Unknown, forgotten I

Nowhere

No-one

Shapeless, spaceless

Oh wait

Oh, shapes

Oh, colours

Unfolding colours

And look—down!

And look—up!

I hold these, I know these

I what?

I who?

Gimme a C

Gimme an A

Up

I fill

I fill space

I spill face

My face

Shapenames

Circles, two

Circles.

I blink

They blink

The hole

the whole of the sky

blinks

reads me

my own

monstrous

I

Gimme an L

Gimme an L

arms, arms move

all the wall

all the wall moves

these, these things, thingers

these flingers

these fingers, move

Gimme a U

no you

only I

only, lonely I have

what have

what have I

done?

Gimme an

"Ehm…"

"*What*?!"

I see a boy, I think. I think, I *am* a boy; a boy is here.

"Ehm, sorry to bother you."

He shouldn't be able to see me. Unless he is me. Is he me?

"I'm a bit lost. I don't know how I got here."

Here is sand. Here is rock and sea, and see, I know here. This is not nowhere, I—

"How can you see me?" I ask. The boy looks confused, and I feel confused. Maybe he *is* me.

"The same way you see me, I suppose," he says, and I do see him, and he's not dressed like me, so maybe he's not me. The sea is thin and slow, and the rocks are thin and soft, and maybe this is not a real place at all.

He's wearing shorts. Big, baggy, khaki shorts. And a white shirt with a collar. I don't think I dress like that. And leather shoes. And thick socks. I definitely don't dress like that.

Everything is ghostly and dim and the ghost of the sea laps on the ghost of the shore.

"I'm…I'm a wee bit scared," says the boy, and he/we look embarrassed, and I'm a bit scared too.

There's a cave, or the ghost of a cave. A big, deep cave in the cliff face and I've been here before, or maybe after. "I was with my friends," the boy goes on, "and we met these…these *things*. Powerful, powerful things! Connor, my friend Connor, he thinks they're amazing, and he's following them round like a puppy. But my other friend, Gordon, he says they're *evil*. I don't think he wants to be friends anymore, not if we carry on meeting these things. And I want my friend Elsa to meet them, but I'm scared of what might happen if she does."

"Oh, yes," I say, "I know them," but I don't know if I'm talking about the things or his friends or all of them together.

"I thought you must," the boy says, "otherwise I don't think I could tell you about them. I don't suppose..." The boy looks sad and scared, and that makes me sad and scared. It's important to me, how this boy feels. This boy feels important to me. "I don't suppose you know what I should do?"

I didn't want to make choices. I didn't want to be asked anymore. I thought I wanted to be forgotten. But I don't think I can forget.

"What do you want to do?" I ask, and the boy throws his hands up, frustrated.

"I want to go back to normal!" he shouts. "Except... I don't. I *really* don't. But I think I could if I decided to. I could forget Things-of-Green. We all could. I could just be me again. And the ground could just be the ground again, the fish and the birds and beasts and the trees, they could just be themselves again and not bother me." A sudden grin, fizzing, excited. "Because, you see, they all *talk* to me now!"

The smile vanishes. Fear reappears. He's only a child. He needs some help. I never thought *he'd* have needed any help.

We stand in silence, and I know this matters. I know it will be difficult for him, knowing Things-of-Green. It will be frightening for the boy, and he won't have many people to ask about it. He will have to navigate a world that is strange to almost everyone he meets.

But if he forgets them, *I* won't have *anyone* to ask about it. I'll never meet them, in fact. And the boy won't be anyone I recognise when next we meet. If we ever even do.

And this isn't a dream. This counts.

How can I tell him not to forget when I only came here to forget myself?

But in the end, it's not really all that hard.

The sand becomes substantial. The water sparks and dances. The grassy clifftop shimmers in the sun.

We pause, the boy and I, and throw pebbles into the water, and the water throws them back, delighted.

"They're incredible, these beings," I tell him. "We need them and they need us." I search my memory for words of comfort. I know how things unfold. "Your friends will get over it all, eventually, and you..."

I look at him, young and healthy and full of uncertainty, and I'm overwhelmed by the possibilities within him. I smile.

"You," I say, "are going to be *amazing*!"

He laughs aloud, delighted, relieved.

"Thanks, laddie!" he says, and is gone.

I am left.

But not alone.

An old man stands where the boy stood.

But it is not the old man I hoped to see.

"You trap yourself in endless, tiring cycles," the old man hisses. "For one brief moment, you were nearly free."

It seems disappointed. It seems angry. I should be afraid of it. It should be afraid of me.

Rant

CALLUM AND THE Other stand on the lonely beach, facing each other in the cold, still air. The old man is hard to look at, as if he's barely really there. Callum feels as if he's looking at someone who was there a moment ago, or who will be there soon, like a bad memory or an imminent threat. His gaze slips off it as if his brain does not really wish to see it. This sensation comes with a deep and rising dread, and Callum realises that he is looking at something completely unnatural. Not unnatural the way he once would have thought of phones or tablets or space stations as unnatural. Compared to this malignant, empty presence, those things might as well grow on trees or be hatched out of eggs. This thing, this being, is not composed of the stuff of life at all; it is an absence of life, or energy, or matter, and how it comes to be standing there is a horror beyond Callum's understanding.

The last time he saw it, it was towering over the Mountain and preparing to devour the world, but here, human-sized and angry, its power seems infinitely more concentrated, and aimed directly at him.

"You fool," it says, the words reaching Callum's ears as if from a great and terrible distance. "You came so close, but you have taken the weak and easy path. You choose to keep things as they are. Suffer all the loss, the hurt, the disappointment. To plunge in this wretched pool and let your pointless ripples spread across the ages, churning and spoiling and endlessly echoing. You could have chosen the perfect silence. You could have had the perfect peace."

Callum, fully back in himself now, looks around for some support. Now would be the perfect moment for Things-of-Green to come flickering around, for Things-of-Water to rise gleeful from the sea, for Elsa to step from the ether, click her fingers and make it all okay. But no help appears.

"I saw it," he says, swallowing down the fear that threatens to silence him. "I saw your perfect peace. And if I'm honest, it wasn't that great." The Other flickers with a dark light, a hole in space and time, and Callum's breath catches in his throat.

"No," it says, "you came close, but you lacked the strength to pass through completely. You are tied here, tied to this vision, captive, helpless. I *know* what you want, Callum Maxwell. You want to know that you will not fail anyone, that you will not hurt anyone, that you will not disappoint anyone. You want to know that your mistakes are erased. You want a decision that cannot be unmade, that can never be proved wrong, whose consequences you will never have to suffer. And yet here you are.

"You had the chance. You could have freed not only yourself, but one you think you love. Instead, you tied him to the rigid, miserable and pointless path he has already trodden infinitely before, and you have tethered yourself, once again, to his fate.

"And this is what will happen from here on. Every careless word of yours will echo on forever. Every thoughtless choice will pile consequence upon consequence. Every wicked thought, however instantly regretted, will grow like a bitter seed. Its roots will break the soil and its thorny branches obscure the sky. The best that you can hope for is that others feel warmly enough towards you to forgive these small catastrophes, but in so doing they will tie themselves to your mess, become less free, and they will lend strength to the evil you have wrought until it spreads unchecked, a cancer in the lives of those it touches.

"And it will touch *every* life.

"I am there, Callum Maxwell. I am at the beginning and end of every trail of events, from the first to the last. What I tell you is the truth. If this world is as connected and intertwined as you have been tricked into believing, how could it be otherwise?"

The figure has changed. It is smaller now, less animated, and its voice is hollow with regret. It seems to be sitting on the sand, its shoulders hunched and huddled, though it is still so difficult to look at that Callum can hardly be sure.

"But what about love?" he asks. "What about the good things I do? The help I can be? How come all these ripples, these echoes...how come they all do harm? What about how happy I am with my friends around me? What about my mum and dad? Am I that terrible that I can only do harm in the world?"

The Other seems to look up, and the sorrow in its voice makes Callum's heart drop to his stomach. It really seems to care.

"Alas," it says, "the greater the good that you attempt, the greater the disappointment when it fails. The brighter the fire that burns, the thinner the ash, my young friend." It rises and moves towards him, and Callum has the ghastly feeling that the very air is rushing out of its way as it approaches.

"I have seen," it says, its voice insinuating and persuasive. "I have seen it all. I see it now. Those creatures you have befriended, they are but glints in the eye, here and gone, while I endure. They are chaos. Mess. Misery. They have no care for you, or anything.

But they will bedevil you for the rest of your days. They will taunt and toy with you, bait you and play with you, and all of that darkness you cast will delight their thoughtless nature.

"It is a *torture* to me, Callum Maxwell, to see you so imprisoned! You, who have come so close to escape. Why must you fight me? Why must you fear me? I only wish to mend the mindless noise, one soul at a time!"

Well, that clinches it. Callum feels his vision clear, his breath come easy and the strength return to his limbs. The figure before him loses its magnetism, loses its dark magic, its cajoling tones now quiet in the thundering of the waves and the whistling wind and the wild cries of wheeling seabirds above.

"But there *is* only one soul," announces Callum, as sure of the truth of it as he has ever been about anything. "Maybe it *will* be you that stills it in the end, but it won't be through any help of mine! Now," he adds, advancing on the tremulous figure before him, feeling a power from his fingertips to the soles of his feet, a light and dancing power that might be Things-of-Green or Things-of-Blood or Things-of-Callum, "why don't ye just *bugger aff*!"

The edges of the sky and the ground and the sea knit themselves together like a healing wound; the wind is cold and fresh on Callum's skin; the cliff is a gothic gateway for the yawning entrance of the Trog's cave; and The Other?

The Other is dispersed among the forgotten and unwanted, never to trouble Callum again.

Music

Now, there is a downside to being the last person standing after a battle with the forces of emptiness, and it is this: the route which took you there may well have lost you the friends and family you most hoped to see when you had won. Callum is old enough not to need to be carried shoulder high and applauded as a hero for this thrilling personal triumph, but as he looks around the windblown beach, he realises just how alone he is.

Elsa, gone. He told her to leave him alone, and she did.

Jenny, gone. Her choice made bravely, she is back where she wants to be, without him.

Things-of-Green, Things-of-Water... Well, were they ever even really here?

But more than all of that, more than any of them, no matter whom he battles, what he decides, where he ends up and how it all ends...

Papa.

Papa really is gone.

"Hello?" he calls. "Is anyone there?" His voice is as quiet and powerless as if he's woken in a silent house in the wee small hours of the night. He paces the sandy beach, reaches the point where sand meets shingle, crunches on for a while. Not a human soul.

"Am I stuck here?" he asks the wind. The kittiwakes on the cliff cackle at him, and a wave slaps a rock and splashes him. It's quite hard not to take it personally.

A squall sets in, a lowering black cloud roiling up over the cliff and dropping a flurry of icy raindrops down upon him. Callum has never been a laddie to mind very much being cold and wet, as long as it's the result of something fun. This isn't much fun, though. In fact, it's pretty terrifying.

Just because I've decided not to forget it all, he thinks, *doesn't mean it hasn't all forgotten me!*

The only shelter in sight is the Trog's cave, so he turns and scrabbles over slippery black rocks to get there. He has to blink the rain from his eyes, and his T-shirt is soaking wet through. With about ten metres to go, he slips and gashes his knee on the rocks, tearing his jeans and drawing blood.

"Aww, come *on*!" he bellows, cursing and swearing in frustration. The wind rises, and more waves break ferociously on the rocks behind him, sending pillars of water into the sky to mingle with the blattering rain.

At last, he makes it to the cave mouth, his eyes unused to the dark, and feels about for a nook he can shelter in. Tangles of wet seaweed meet his questing hand, and he slithers about blindly for a while till he finds a neat little alcove set back from the vigorous weather.

And there he sits, feeling completely sorry for himself, listening to the booming waves and the sounds of a world that seems to have no need for him.

He realises he doesn't even know when this is. Is he stuck in the past? In some far-distant future? Have all his adventures already happened, or are they a script as yet unwritten? Perhaps, as Elsa once said, he is outside of time altogether, which probably doesn't bode too well for the happy reunions his mind keeps teasing him with.

"Well, this might be it, I suppose," he says aloud. And perhaps not so bad at that. After all, the Trog lived in this cave for decades and seemed pretty happy on it. *Very* happy, in fact. A bit maniacal. But that won't matter if there's no-one around to criticise him.

His mind starts wandering over what there might be to eat in a place like this, and it's really not too shabby. There's plenty of shellfish. Seaweed's edible, he thinks. And hey, fresh water just falls out of the sky! A fire would be good, but he'll figure that out. Then he thinks about sitting by a fire on the beach, all alone, and it not mattering if it's a good fire or a rotten fire or if it's a nice night or a miserable night, because there is no-one there to share it with, and he bursts into uncontrollable, wracking, hopeless tears.

For a short while, he is simply lost in unhappiness, wordlessly wailing, clenching his fists, clutching his hair and shaking. When the sound first meets his ears, he assumes it's his own cries echoing back from the depths of the cave. The sound is certainly as sad as he is, and it rises and falls with his own. But when he catches his breath and blinks away the tears, the sound remains, mournful and keening. Is it the wind?

The melody repeats. Wind does not usually do that. It is slow, low, rhythmic. It is music.

Music coming from deep within the cave.

With nothing to lose and with barely a thought, Callum takes a deep breath, stands and gropes his way deep into the dark. In places, the passage is so narrow he has to stand on tiptoe and edge sideways to squeeze through, but the strange, rippling music draws him on. It could be a flute; it is haunting and human and it winds through the passageway, lamenting, flowing, grace notes glinting off the slow, sad song.

Callum reaches the end of the passage, and it opens into a cavernous space, pitch-black and still but for the swirling, skirling, insistent sound. If it had been a single flute in the narrow space, here it is a chorus, a choir, a hundred echoing voices drawing him on. It grows so intense it prickles his skin, and he continues, led through the dark by this rising wash of sound, tumultuous, desperate, demanding, and Callum goes on till he can go no further, pressed against the black wall of the cave. The stone is vibrating, ringing, chiming with the strength of it, buzzing against his palms as he feels his way along, an electric charge flowing right up his arms. The melody rises, shrill, almost painful, but full of such longing and loss that it folds itself into his very bones.

It flows through him till he is one with the rock, one with the air, one with cliff and cave and ocean. All the little tortures he's been playing through his mind are gone, lifted away, spun into song, the deep and the dark, the high and the bright, the rhythm a heartbeat as big as the Mountain itself.

A crack appears in the wall of the cave. Too narrow at first to be sure—maybe the light is just his eyes playing tricks on him—it seems as if the sound is becoming louder, as if it might be coming through the crack, which widens to a finger-width, and there's no mistaking it. The music is coming from somewhere beyond it.

Callum runs his hands over the rough edges. He can fit them in the crack now, and the fizz and tingle of the music grows till it is almost unbearable. He braces his feet on the stony ground and fumbles around until he has a good, strong grip. Then, without knowing why, and surely pointlessly, he grits his teeth and *pulls* at the crack.

The tempo increases, trilling like a skylark, encouraging, cajoling, lending strength to his ridiculous efforts. He grunts and heaves and yes! *Yes!* The crack widens! Callum shifts his hands to a better position, bends his knees, gets his shoulder right into it and *strains* at the widening light. The music is gleeful, celebratory. It's working. *It's working!* In a moment, Callum will be able to squeeze right into the crack and through, through into the light!

But what for? What then?

More of the same? Back to a bleak, shrunken Skerrils? People changing, leaving? Back to choices he lacks the wisdom to make?

The music stops, leaving only a ringing in his ears. He is stuck in the crack, and the crack begins to close.

Rock walls are easing shut around him. He feels the weight, the crushing, irresistible weight of stone. What a fool he'd been to think he could overcome it! Silly, silly wee boy.

No more decisions.

No more choices.

The end?

Don't be ridiculous.

A hand grabs his arm from the other side of the crack and pulls and pulls and *pulls*, and Callum yells in alarm, his voice unbearably loud in this tight and shrinking space, but the hand, the hand—it will not let him go! He thinks his arm will be wrenched from his shoulder, but still he is pulled, dragged, *hauled* until he starts to move again, sliding and scraping through the diminishing crack and ow ow ow ow *ow ow OOOWWWWWWW*

and

OUT!

And out.

Really out. Fresh air. Sunlight. The real world.

"About time, you daftie," says Vicky, still holding his arm in one hand, her flute in the other. She is red-faced and breathless, but smiling. "You didn't think I'd forget you, did you?" And she hugs him, and he hugs her, and he's home.

Close

THEY ARE AT the entrance to the Tinkers' Cave, right where Jenny disappeared, a good four miles through the Mountain from the Trog's cave where Callum thought he was, and a couple of miles more from the town. They let each other go after a few speechless minutes, Callum clearing his throat in mild embarrassment, Vicky raising an eyebrow then laughing.

"You saved me," is all that Callum can think of to say.

"You'd have got out eventually," she answers. "But you know, Callum, you don't have to do everything on your own."

The sun is low in the autumn afternoon, and a fresh breeze ruffles the heather and grass at their feet. They turn, their shadows stretching off behind them, and head back towards Skerrils like any two pals out for a daunder. Callum is more grateful than he can say, not only that Vicky came for him but that he doesn't need to try explaining what's been going on. She understands without the need for any storytelling. She's humming a wee tune to herself as they walk, tapping a rhythm on the keys of her flute, perfectly content just to be there.

"Vicky," says Callum as Skerrils comes into view, all amber and bronze in the early sunset colours. He pauses. He has a question but doesn't want to discover that he won't be able to ask it. He has been here before, after all, and it drove him near demented. His first adventure with Things-of-Green had ended in forgetfulness, his triumph bathed in loss and confusion. But he takes a breath and tries.

"Vicky, do you remember Things-of-Green?" He knows at once from the fact that he can ask, the fact that his tongue is not tied in that irksome enchantment, that of course she does remember, and she is happy to confirm it.

"I do," she says. "It took a little while, but I do."

"And don't you miss that magic? Living so far from Skerrils?"

"No, I don't, Callum. I don't because that magic's not only *in* Skerrils."

This stops Callum in his tracks, and Vicky pauses to wait for him.

"What," he says, "you're telling me that Things-of-Green isn't just here?"

Vicky gives him a patient nod. "Of course not. She's everywhere."

"*She?*"

"Well, *they*, I suppose. I see them as female, but I guess you don't. It's hardly the weirdest thing about them, though, is it?"

Callum has to acknowledge the truth of this, though he's still banjaxed at the thought of these things anywhere but here. Vicky sees his confusion.

"We carry them with us, Callum," she says. "We carry a lot of things with us when we leave a place like this. For what it's worth, I carry *you* with me too, you know."

They walk on, the town growing before them, and Callum sees it as both a place and a time, built on centuries of memory, running on endless possibilities.

"Will I see them again?"

"Maybe. If you want to. You might not need to now, though, I suppose."

The light dulls in the cloudless sky, their shadows stretch and fade,
    and Skerrils
    welcomes two old friends
    back
    into its peaceful embrace.

*   *   *

ALAN McClure

Behind them, far behind them, on the wild, cold mountainside, an old woman steps lightly through the gorse and heather, her silver hair cascading down her back in the breeze. She turns and casts a final look at the distant lights of Skerrils, smiles and fades from sight as the Mountain silhouettes against a blue-black canopy of stars.

Epilogue

AND WHAT OF me, dear reader? Me, the nameless voice who has led you on this merry dance? The story is Callum's, but it was my job to tell it, and for now, at least, it is told. Where, then, do I go?

There is more I would like to know. I would like to know what Jenny remembers. I would like to know if she and Callum remain friends—or become more than friends.

I would like to know what Callum can say to his mother. Can you imagine that reunion? I suspect he can say what he chooses, now there is no magic to restrain him, but will he risk the consequences of reminding her of Elsa, the mother she has forgotten? Dare he set those ripples in motion?

You know, I'm even a wee bit worried about Wullie and Brian. I'm sure they'll be fine, mind.

There is always more—more to learn, more to tell—but all things have their time, and I've had mine. I could not have had it without you, and for that, I will be forever grateful.

Perhaps one day you'll think of the road we've taken, and you'll lift this tale again, set out from the beginning. But it won't be the same. It can't ever be the same. You will have changed, and whatever changes are in you must also be in me, within the world we weave together. It's even possible that I will tell you completely different things if you hazard this journey again. And in telling them anew, I will be something other than what I have been. There are as many versions of each of us as there are people to see us, each with its own truth, its own value.

Memories change. Some fade, some mature; some grow unbearably intense, but none can be lived again. That is both the sadness and the sweetness of this life.

I will, if I may, remember you. I hope you'll do the same for me, one voice among many, who once shared a precious space inside your mind. You will go forward and grow as our time together fades like a glowing sunset on a lowering October evening.

Perhaps, just perhaps, there is a place where we all will meet again.

But for now,

dear friend,

goodbye.

The end.

Acknowledgements

I'd no intention of writing a sequel to *Callum and the Mountain* until pupils Crossmichael Primary School, who were studying the book with their teacher Ros Stevens, convinced me that a return to Skerrils was necessary. Huge thanks to them, and to my own classes at Kirkcudbright Primary, who saw things in the first book that made the second one possible.

Debbie McGowan, a tireless and dedicated publisher, editor and all-round excellent human, once again hammered a sketchy manuscript into a lovely shiny book, for which I'm eternally grateful.

As well as being a crazy adventure, this is a book about overcoming grief, confusion and loss of purpose, written in a time when great swathes of humanity were struggling with these very issues. Being blessed with my pals and my incredible family meant that love and hope were always going to be the answer, as indeed they turned out to be. Shell, Fergus and Robin, this one, like every one, is for you.

About the Author

Alan McClure is a writer and musician based in Galloway, south-west Scotland. His creative output is eclectic and prolific, encompassing oral storytelling, poetry, songs, novels, short stories and audio sketches. He is a founding member of Lost Wasp Records, singer and chief songwriter with Alan & the Big Hand, occasional member of The Wee Folk Storytellers and a solo performer of growing repute. He is also a primary school teacher, a job which provides constant inspiration and ample opportunity for explaining and discovering through stories and songs.

By the Author

Medica Britanimalicum (Blurb, 2011)

Ross Bay and Other Poems (Blurb, 2011)

The Choices of Molly Fortune (Amazon, 2014)

Alternative Endings and Other Poems (Amazon 2014)

Callum and the Mountain

Jack's Well

Callum and The Other

Other examples of Alan's music and writing can be found at www.alanmcclure.co.uk

Beaten Track Publishing

For more titles from Beaten Track Publishing,
please visit our website:

https://www.beatentrackpublishing.com

Thanks for reading!